—MYSTERY AT—
Jacob's Well

MARCIA ALLEN BENNETT
ILLUSTRATED BY JASON C. ECKHARDT

EAKIN PRESS ⨏ Austin, Texas

DEDICATED

To the memory of our son John
and
To the memory of those who died
so tragically in Jacob's Well

CONTENTS

vi

AUTHOR'S NOTE

Jacob's Well in Wimberley and Wonder Cave in San Marcos are actual places in Texas. The Jacob's Well area was once inhabited by the Tonkawa tribe of American Indians.

Sadly, eight divers are indeed known to have lost their lives in Jacob's Well. All other characters and events in the story, however, are fiction.

ACKNOWLEDGMENTS

My heartfelt thanks . . .

To my loving husband, Bill, for his patience, his encouragement, and his editing skills;

To my incredible family for their enduring love and support;

To David Baker, executive director of the Wimberley Valley Watershed Association, for his tireless efforts to preserve Jacob's Well and for his encouragement in the writing of this book;

To Hays County Justice of the Peace Andy Cable and Sheriff's Deputy Darrell Ayers for their information on Jacob's Well;

To Kathy and Dan Misiaszek, Jacob's Well divers, for their technical evaluation.

CHAPTER 1
Divers in Danger

Four divers were deep below the surface of Jacob's Well. Their plan was to explore and map the series of underwater chambers that lay 130 feet beneath the ground. Above them a silent and anxious cluster of people waited in the damp, chilled air.

Thirteen-year-old Mike Tracey was one of those standing and waiting beside the well. The divers' extra tanks lay not far from his feet.

Mike absently watched the tanks as moisture from the foggy winter mist formed glistening droplets on their cold metal sides. The droplets rolled slowly down and under the tanks to puddle on the rock surface beneath. To Mike, the extra tanks were a grim reminder that the air supply of the divers was limited.

His twin sister's voice broke into his thoughts as she whispered, "Mike, look! Over there behind us.

What is that?" Mike could hear his own anxiety reflected in Hannah's voice.

"Do you see it, Mike? Those bubbles. Where are they coming from?"

Mike's eyes followed the direction of her hand. In the distance he saw a wavering line of bubbles moving slowly up the creek, eerily creeping further and further away from the well.

"Mike, are those from the divers? What does it mean? The bubbles are so far from the well where the divers went down."

Mike heard the fear in his sister's voice. He tried to sound confident and reassuring when he spoke to her.

"Hannah," he answered in a whisper, "I think the bubbles are from the divers' air tanks and it's probably all right. Don't forget, the caves go upcreek from the well. So probably the divers have just gone a little bit further back in the caves."

Hannah said only, "Oh." She, too, felt the apprehension which penetrated the fog and seeped into the soul of each person present. She knew the underwater caves were deep, and that the divers were now over a hundred feet below the surface, making their way through the dark and narrow water passageways.

"Don't worry, Hannah. I'm sure the divers are okay." Mike shivered, chilled by the dampness.

Her voice hushed, Hannah spoke again. "Mike, who are those people on top of the cliff?"

Mike's eyes were drawn to the rocky bluff overlooking Jacob's Well. Four people stood like sentinels atop the cliff. Silent and solemn in the gray drizzle, they looked like apparitions conjured up in someone's mind. The unmoving figures held lighted candles which flickered eerily in the dimness of the fog.

Mike knew why they were there. They had felt moved to be present today to honor the memories of eight young men—the eight men who had died over the years exploring the underwater caves of Jacob's Well. And now Mike shared the fear of the onlookers, that there could be another tragedy, another life claimed by the well.

"Hannah, the people on the cliff are here in memory of those who have died in the well."

"Oh, Mike, that's, that's..." Hannah's voice dropped to a low murmur. "That's a beautiful thing to do."

"Yeah," said Mike. "I think so, too." To himself he said softly, "I just hope and pray there's not another accident today."

Mike glanced at the orange nylon rope which

snaked its way down deep into the well. Mike knew the rope was a guideline the divers could follow back up to the surface. But it seemed to him that already too much time had passed since the divers entered the well.

Frightening questions kept running through Mike's mind. Where were the divers? Why didn't they surface? Had there been yet another tragedy in the frightening and fascinating depths of Jacob's Well?

Mike shivered again. He pulled his windbreaker tight around him and pushed his hands into the pockets. He tried to tell himself he was shivering from the cold dampness. But it was more than that. He felt a gnawing fear seeping into his mind, and it was not only for the divers. It was a day just like this that the ghost... Stop it, he told himself.

Mike tried to laugh off the strange feeling. "Good day for the old ghost, isn't it, Hannah? I almost expect him to show up any minute."

"Mike, I don't know what you are talking about," Hannah whispered. "What ghost?"

Mike spoke quietly. "The ghost of Gray Wolf, of course. Hannah, I have never been out here in weather like this. It's so, so... well, ghostly with the fog and mist. I almost expect to see Gray Wolf at any minute."

"Who is Gray Wolf?" asked Hannah, a puzzled look on her face.

"I'll tell you about it later," whispered Mike, not wanting to upset his sister. But Mike couldn't get the thought of the ghost out of his mind.

This was exactly the kind of day that the ghost of the old Tonkawa chief, Gray Wolf, was said to appear. Mike told himself he didn't believe there were such things as ghosts. And yet his Great Uncle Ezra, an honest and reliable man, had claimed to have seen the ghost. Mike forced his mind back to reality and looked at the scene around the well.

On the other side of the wide creek an ambulance was parked on the dirt trail, emergency medical personnel standing ready beside it. Their faces were sober and concerned. They knew the danger of the well.

Jacob's Well had a history that Mike did not like to think about. He had been coming to the well to swim for many years. However, it was only recently, at age thirteen, that he had felt any sense of danger, a very real awareness of what could happen in the well.

Growing up in the small village of Wimberley, Texas, generations of young people and their elders alike had enjoyed swimming in Jacob's Well. It was a good place for a summer outing, easy to get to, not far from the village itself. And it was beautiful. Mike could understand why the Tonkawa tribe had considered Jacob's Well a sacred place.

The well itself, with an opening between ten and fifteen feet in diameter, spewed forth crystal water with a pressure so strong you could not sink in it. To submerge yourself at all was a challenge.

Even in the hottest of Texas summers, the water, gushing up from caves and caverns deep below the surface, had an arctic iciness that shocked the swimmers plunging into its sparkling clear surface.

Jacob's Well was a wonderful place, a place for fun and picnics and happy times. But now Mike felt the peril of the well and saw it differently.

"Mike," said Hannah, "I wish the divers would come up. I keep imagining one of them getting trapped down there, stuck in one of those narrow places. It scares me. In fact I wonder if maybe we shouldn't have come."

"Yeah, Hannah, I wonder about that, too. About our coming today, I mean. I just thought it would be something interesting to do, seeing the divers going down to map the caves underneath. When Grandpa asked us if we would like to come out with him, I was more than ready. It sounded exciting." Mike paused thoughtfully. "But I wasn't prepared for the way I feel."

The dreariness of the day descended even more

heavily on Mike. He took off his glasses and once more wiped them on his shirttail to remove the moisture.

Usually Mike was struck by the untamed natural beauty of Jacob's Well. But today? Today, with the water reflecting only ghostly gray mists, the tree limbs hanging wet and still, the cliff towering over them menacingly, Jacob's Well seemed ominous and threatening.

Mike stared at the well. The orange rope was the only connection, the only thread between the divers and the people waiting above.

Mike tried to will the rope to move, to give them all some sign that the divers were all right, that they were on their way to the surface. How long could they safely stay down there? He wished he had asked someone that before the divers went down.

At that moment something in the water caught his eye. Was the rope moving, or was it his imagination?

"Hannah, look! The rope is moving. I think they are coming up."

"Thank goodness," said Hannah, as she watched bubbles begin to rise from the divers' tanks to the surface of the well.

Soon a diver appeared just below the surface of the well's water. One by one the divers began emerging from the well, their masked faces breaking through the silvery sheen of the water's surface. Relief was apparent on the faces of those watching as the last diver climbed from the well.

"Now I can look forward to seeing the videotape they've been making down there," said Hannah to her brother. "Knowing they are all out safely sure is a big relief."

"Yeah," said Mike. "I feel like I can breathe again. I guess our imaginations were working pretty hard for a while, what with the danger and all the things that could be going wrong."

The divers spoke quietly to several people who seemed to be in charge of the exploration. Then the divers began to remove their equipment and pack it up. The underwater camcorder was carefully stowed in a box. Lights, tanks, flippers, masks, and wet suits were put into the back of a covered pickup truck. Three of the four divers got into the truck and drove away.

The EMS attendants climbed into their ambulance and drove off through the drizzle, windshield wipers slapping back and forth rhythmically. Mike and Hannah watched as the candle bearers disappeared into the woods above the cliff.

—CHAPTER 2—
The Figure at the Well

The area surrounding Jacob's Well now seemed strangely quiet and deserted, its sounds muted by the rain. Hannah and Mike stood silently in the misty rain, waiting for their grandfather as he questioned the diver who emerged last. Their grandfather was gathering information for an article he was writing for the local newspaper.

"Mike," said Hannah, "tell me more about the ghost while we wait for Grandpa. Who is Gray Wolf?"

"He's an American Indian, chief of the tribe that used to live here. Don't you remember the story?"

"No, I don't remember any story. Mike, I have no idea what you are talking about. I never heard of Gray Wolf. And besides that, I thought we were supposed to call them 'Native Americans.'"

"I thought so, too, Hannah, until I started looking up stuff about different tribes on the Internet. On their own web sites they called themselves Indians so much that I looked up the web site of the Bureau of Indian Affairs. I learned that the preferred term now is American Indian."

"Why?" asked Hannah.

"They explained that it's because Hawaiians and other South Pacific people were included in the term 'Native Americans.' The American Indians wanted a term all their own."

"That's interesting," said Hannah, "but I want to know more about the ghost."

"Don't you remember the story about the ghost Great Uncle Ezra said he saw out here?"

"No," said Hannah. "I still have no idea what you are talking about."

"I know you must have heard the story, Hannah. I'll ask Grandpa to tell us again on the way home. It was on a misty day like this when Great Uncle Ezra said he saw the ghost, but other people say they have seen it, too. Always on misty, foggy days just like this."

"Has anyone seen this thing, this ghost, recently?" asked Hannah, looking around apprehensively.

"Last year, two people camping beside the creek swear they saw it," Mike answered. "The campers were sitting just inside the opening of their tent, looking out at the misty rain and wishing it would stop.

"Then all of a sudden they saw a tribal chief in native dress standing on that rock just over there. He looked old, with a wrinkled face. His face had black lines on it, so he must have been a Tonkawa. Tonkawa tribe members tattooed their faces and bodies.

"Anyway, for a while the old warrior just stood and looked at them. Then he raised one arm very slowly and seemed to be beckoning for them to come closer. They were too scared to move, but if they could have moved, they would have run fast in the other direction. Suddenly, right before their eyes, the figure vanished, just disappeared."

Hannah shivered as she looked at the rock where the ghost had stood.

Mike and Hannah's grandfather finished his interview and motioned for them to head to the car. The twins began walking toward their grandfather's ancient jeep, Hannah almost trotting to keep up with her long-legged brother.

Although they were twins, Mike and Hannah couldn't be more different in appearance. Many of their classmates didn't even realize they were related, much less twins. Mike was lanky and thin. Most of the time his glasses were sliding down his nose. "I'm too busy to keep getting them adjusted all the time," he would say.

His dark hair seemed to follow his glasses in the downward slide, for it often hung down over his left eyebrow. Some people thought of him as a nerd and Hannah sometimes teased him with the name, but she was proud of his bright mind and his interest in so many things.

Hannah was shorter than her brother and had a round face framed by straight blond hair. When she was little she wore it in long braids. Mike said she looked like the little Dutch girl in one of their story-books.

Hannah got into the front seat of her grandpa's old jeep while Mike climbed over some fishing gear and into the back seat. Grandpa started the engine, and the jeep wound its way up the muddy trail beside Cypress Creek.

"Grandpa," Hannah said, "I want to know about the ghost Great Uncle Ezra saw at Jacob's Well. The one Mike calls Gray Wolf."

"You know, Hannah," said Grandpa, "it's funny you should ask about Gray Wolf. I was thinking about him while we were waiting for the divers to surface. Guess it's the weather. This kind of weather, all chilly and misty, is the kind of weather when old Gray Wolf likes to show up."

"That's what Mike said. Was it gray and drizzly

like this when Great Uncle Ezra saw the ghost of Gray Wolf?"

"Yep, sure was. Here's the story just like Uncle Ezra told it to me a long time ago before he died.

"Seems Uncle Ezra and his best friend, Rufus Caldwell, had come out to the well to do a little fishing. They really didn't expect to catch much in the way of fish, but it was a good excuse to come out to the well. They were just boys, about your age—thirteen, fourteen, somewhere in there—and they had ridden out to the well on their horses.

"Back then, your great-great-grandpa, Ezra's pa, had a pretty good-sized spread out in this direction. They had some cattle, horses, other animals.

"Anyway, to get on with the story about the ghost, Uncle Ezra and Rufus were sitting on the bank by the creek. It was just about the same spot where the ambulance was parked today. The weather was pretty fair when the boys first got out to the well, but the sky began to cloud up. First thing you know, it was misty raining, a cold drizzling foggy rain just like today.

"But the boys didn't want to go home yet. There were chores waiting for them at home and it was nice and comfortable sitting at the creek holding a fishing pole, and talking, and sometimes not talking at all.

"The misting got worse and it began to get foggy.

All of a sudden, Rufus says in a voice you could hardly hear cause he was so scared. He says, 'Ezra, there's a thing over there, standing on that rock.' That's what he called it, 'a thing,' because it didn't look like anything he had ever seen before."

Mike and Hannah were hardly daring to breathe as they heard Grandpa's story.

"Uncle Ezra told me himself that it was the scariest thing he ever saw in his life. He said at first it was just a thick, misty, elongated form he saw. Then it began to take on more of a shape and it began to look like a man.

"'Ezra, do you see it?' Rufus whispered. He clutched Ezra's arm. 'Tell me what you see.' Rufus was almost begging.

"Uncle Ezra didn't know if he could speak, he was so scared himself, so he just nodded at first. Then he told Rufus in a kind of croaking voice, 'Rufus, what I see can't be real. It just can't be. I see an Indian standing right there on that rock.'

" 'That's it, Ezra,' Rufus said. 'That's what I see, too. But I sure don't want to be seeing it.'

"Uncle Ezra told me that right then the ghostly figure raised up his right arm real slow-like, turned his palm up, and beckoned to those boys to come over to where he was standing.

"At first, Ezra and Rufus couldn't move a muscle. Then Rufus jumped up like he was shot from a cannon and ran over to the horses. Uncle Ezra said Rufus was in that saddle and had his horse flying down that trail before Ezra even got to his horse— and he wasn't exactly dragging his feet.

"Uncle Ezra said he looked over at the rock as he rode off and watched that Indian just disappear. That ghost didn't walk off anywhere, he just vanished into thin air.

"Well, it was a long time before Uncle Ezra went back out to Jacob's Well. Or Rufus either. And neither one of them ever went back out there on a rainy day, not as long as they lived."

"Wow," said Hannah. "What a spooky story! No wonder you were watching for Gray Wolf's ghost today, Mike. I don't think I much want to come out here again on a rainy day either."

"I don't want to come out here on another gray, rainy day like today," said Mike, "but I would like to come back out here and explore a little more, maybe learn some more about the Tonkawas."

Hannah and Mike were quiet for a moment. Then Mike asked, "Grandpa, why does everyone call the ghost 'Gray Wolf?'"

"Mike," answered his grandpa, "I don't know the

true story of how the ghost got that name. But I did hear that the Tonkawas once had a chief named Gray Wolf who was killed by some renegade Comanches."

Grandpa continued. "I read somewhere that when one of the tribe died and the three-day mourning period was over, no one was ever again allowed to speak the name of the dead man. They believed if you did you would make his spirit angry and he would come back to bother the living. Maybe someone spoke Gray Wolf's name."

"*Hmm,*" said Mike.

Hannah turned around in her seat in the jeep and looked at her brother. "Uh-oh," she said. "I know that *hmm* sound. I feel trouble coming on. You're plotting something, and whatever it is I have a bad feeling about it."

Mike laughed.

"I'm not kidding, Mike. If it's something to do with Jacob's Well or that ghost, I think you should forget it."

CHAPTER 3
Four for Adventure

"Hey, Hannah," yelled Mike, tossing his backpack on the kitchen counter. "Where are you?"

"Sarah and I are upstairs," called his twin sister, "and you don't have to bellow at me. I can hear you three blocks away."

Mike clomped up the stairs two at a time, his glasses bouncing on his nose. "Hi, Sarah," Mike said, giving a yank to Sarah's long hair.

Sarah was Hannah's best friend and spent a lot of time at Mike and Hannah's house. She had been Hannah's closest friend since kindergarten. Hannah was usually the one to think up activities for the two of them, and Sarah happily followed along, her petite dark-haired figure a striking contrast to Hannah's blond roundness.

Mike continued, his voice betraying his excitement. "I just wanted to tell you guys that I talked to

Mrs. Jameson about our science project. She gave us the okay. She liked your idea, Hannah, about combining our community ecology and cleanup program with a study of local caves. We can make Jacob's Well the focal point in our report." Mike pushed his glasses up on the bridge of his nose. "I think it will be a great project and lots of fun."

"Me, too," replied Hannah. "I've gotten over being scared about Jacob's Well," she confessed. "Maybe I'm still a little nervous, but I think working out at the well could be fun. And with Luis and Sarah on the team to share the work, it shouldn't be too hard to get everything done."

Mike propped himself against the doorframe of Hannah's room. "I think we should get started on our project right away," he told the girls. "I have already talked to David Maynor, the guy in charge of Jacob's Well education center. He's got a project lined up for us there."

Sarah was excited, too. "Jacob's Well will be a perfect place to begin our project," she agreed. "I've heard a lot of stories about it; some of them were mysterious and spooky. You and Hannah told me about the underwater caves at the well."

"Yeah," said Mike enthusiastically. "Finding out more about the caves can be part of our report. Let's

18

call Luis and all plan to go out to the well on Saturday."

Luis, Mike's best friend, was a shyer version of Mike. Like Mike, he was tall and long-legged, but quieter and more thoughtful. Both enjoyed sports, especially basketball. This school year was the first time Mike, Hannah, Luis, and Sarah had found themselves in the same class. Mike, especially, loved science and was pleased that he, his sister, and their two friends could work on a project together.

"Saturday sounds good to me," said Sarah.

"Mike," said Hannah, "why don't you go call Luis right now? If he can go on Saturday we can ride out to Jacob's Well on our bikes and look around."

— CHAPTER 4 —

To the Well

Saturday found the four friends energetically pedaling their bicycles along the narrow, hilly road leading to Jacob's Well. Toward the bottom of a steep hill, Mike slowed his bike.

"We're almost there," he called back to his friends, who were enjoying the easy downhill finish to their ride. "I can see from here that the gate is open. Good thing Mr. Bartle remembered to unlock it for us."

"I thought David Maynor owned the well," said Sarah.

"Mr. Bartle and David both do," explained Mike. "David owns the property on the other side of the creek and Mr. Bartle owns this side. This side is closer for us and easier to ride our bikes to."

Luis was just behind Mike, but slowed as they neared the entrance to Jacob's Well. "There's something creepy about this place," Luis muttered to himself, slowing his bike to a crawl. "Probably just my imagination. But still..."

Hannah pedaled past Luis and Mike to go through the gate first, then followed the dirt trail that ran beside the shallow creek. She hopped off her bike and propped it against a gnarled, old oak tree.

"Hurry up," she called to her friends as they rode their bikes into the clearing. "I'm starving! Let's eat." Hannah hung her bike helmet on the handlebars. She removed her backpack and began rummaging through it to retrieve her lunch and water bottle.

"Wow," exclaimed Luis, braking his bike abruptly. "I never saw anyplace like this. This is awesome!"

Sarah dumped her bike next to Hannah's. "Hey, you guys, I'm with Hannah. Let's eat!"

To Luis, she said, "I can't believe you have never been out here before. But then, you haven't lived in Wimberley as long as we have. I guess sometimes it takes a while before you hear about places like this."

Luis dropped his bike on the ground and walked through the stubble of weedy grass, dry and hard from the winter's cold. He stepped over to the edge of the clear, gently flowing creek. Turning slowly, he stared at the area surrounding Jacob's Well.

"I don't see anything that looks like a well," he

mumbled to himself. "And I still think there's something creepy about this place."

Luis gazed across the creek where the large limestone boulders protruded from the hillside, looming over the area and forming the steep cliff overlooking the creek's path.

The creek bed was about twenty-five feet wide, but the creek itself was narrower and only several inches deep because of the drought that was now parching this part of Texas. Luis looked for the well, which was supposed to be right in the middle of the creek.

"Hey, Mike," he called over his shoulder. "Where's that famous well?"

Mike walked over to stand beside Luis. "Look there," he said, pointing toward the rock face. "It's in the middle of the creek between us and that rock shelf."

"Oh, yeah, I think I see it now," replied Luis. "My gosh, if that is the well I see, it's huge!"

"Yeah," answered Mike. "The opening at the top of the well is about ten feet wide. Neat place for a science project, huh?" Mike paused, then said, "Even if she is my sister, I have to admit that Hannah came up with a good idea this time. We combine our community cleanup and beautification work with our science project and have fun at the same time."

"I first heard of Jacob's Well right after we moved

to Wimberley," said Luis, "but I thought it was private property and nobody could come out here."

Mike answered, "Mr. Bartle owns the property that runs along one side of the creek. He has agreed to let us enter the Jacob's Well property through his ranch gate in exchange for doing some cleaning up and improvement of the area. That's where Hannah got the idea."

Serendipity, Sarah had called it.

Luis looked around again, this time more carefully. "I don't see any garbage or trash to pick up around here. How are we going to beautify a place that looks clean as a whistle?"

"Truth is," answered Mike, "we may not find much trash here right now because the weather is still pretty cold. Not many people are out here this time of year, but come spring, the messer-uppers will come."

Mike gazed at the rock formations and at the crystal water. "Hard to believe people could trash up a place like this. The water in Jacob's Well is said to be the cleanest water anywhere around. Sometimes just a short way downstream the water will have a fecal coliform count of 830 colonies per 100 milliliters of water. Here at Jacob's Well it will be a count of only two. The higher the count, the more it indicates the presence of pathogens and other bacteria."

Hannah poked Sarah and rolled her eyes. The girls giggled.

"What?" said Mike. "Why is that funny?"

"It's not funny, Mike," answered Hannah. "It's just that you always have some weird facts or statistics to add to whatever we're talking about. I don't know how you remember all that stuff."

Mike tossed a pebble into the stream. "Well, don't forget," he continued, "this place may look okay now, but keeping the grounds cleaned up isn't a one-time event. We promised to stick to this project at least until school starts again next year!"

"Come on, you guys," said Sarah. "You can gaze at the water later. Let's eat and then we can explore some."

The boys dug around in their backpacks and brought out long, fat sandwiches filled with meats, cheeses, tomatoes, pickles, and strips of bell pepper.

"Hey, not fair," said Hannah. "You cheated and bought those at the sandwich shop! 'Just bring a snack from home,' you told us. Sarah and I might as well not have bothered to make our lunches. You have enough for ten people."

"Yeah," answered Mike with a grin. "You know how it is with us men."

Hannah looked at Sarah and grinned. "Yeah, right. Men."

"You know," commented Luis, his eyes fixed on the well in the center of the creek, "there's something strange about this place. The well itself, for instance. You could walk by here and not really notice it."

Luis pulled his jacket tighter around him. "I don't care how chilly the weather is today, I'm going to take my shoes off after lunch and wade over to the well. I want a closer look. It's just so strange to have water bubbling up like that out of nowhere."

"Good gosh, Luis," said Mike as he stuffed another chunk of sandwich into his mouth. "Haven't you ever seen a well before?"

"Sure, I've seen wells before, but they always looked like the pictures of wishing wells you see in books. None of them looked like this."

Mike began munching on an apple. "True, you probably haven't seen one like this before. The water in this well comes up from underground caves down in the Trinity aquifer. And it doesn't just ooze up. It's like a large and very powerful spring. It gushes up with plenty of force behind it and pours out thousands of gallons a minute. Local historians say that a long time ago the water in the well sometimes shot up in a geyser twenty feet high."

"Wow!" Luis was impressed. "It's hard to imagine that much water coming out, isn't it?"

"Yeah," said Mike. "My dad says back when he was a kid there was a spot in the creek about twenty-five yards away where the water shot up three or four feet high in the fault line."

Mike pointed. "See that crack in the rock in the creekbed? Right over there, that long crack in the rock."

"Yeah," said Luis. "What about it?

"That's the fault line. You guys probably know about faults. They are ruptures in the rocks where the earth's tectonic plates have shifted. The rocks get squeezed and they crack."

"I remember reading something about those plates," said Hannah.

Sarah finished her sandwich and took a long drink from her water bottle. "Mike," she said, "you're our team leader for the science project. I'm not totally clear on our assignment. Just what are we supposed to do and where do we start?"

"Well," answered Mike, "we've been studying geology and cave formations in science class, so I'm hoping we can combine regular underground caves and underwater caves for our report. In addition to that, we can work some of our ecology and preservation efforts into our report."

Mike continued, "I'm hoping we can get a speaker, too. Maybe somebody can come from the Texas Cave Management Association, and also we can get somebody from Texas Rope Rescue or from SMART."

"What in the world is *smart?*" asked Sarah.

"It's S-M-A-R-T. Those letters stand for the San Marcos Area Recovery Team. They are the ones who do rescue work at places like Jacob's Well, and it was their divers who were exploring and mapping the well a while back."

"Brother Mike," said Hannah, "I have to admit it. I am impressed! Where did you get all those ideas?"

"Good old Internet," answered Mike.

"I might have known," said Hannah with a sigh. "That's why I never get a chance to use the computer."

CHAPTER 5
Fighting the Fear

Luis finished his sandwich and stood up. He walked over to the edge of the creek, where he sat down and rolled up the legs of his jeans.

"Here I go," he called to the others, "about to freeze my feet off, but I have got to get a better look at that well." He removed his shoes and socks.

Luis hesitantly stuck one foot in the water. "Yikes," he shouted, jerking his foot out. "That's the coldest water I ever felt. I think I'd better do this gradually."

After keeping both feet in the water for a few minutes, Luis waded over to the well's edge. The water was crystal clear even deep down in the well. Luis thought he could see the bottom many feet below.

The rim of the well itself was several inches underwater and level with the creek bed, giving the well an unreal appearance. Standing at the edge of the opening, Luis stared down and caught his breath. "My gosh," he said almost reverently, "this is fantastic. I wonder how many feet to the bottom."

Overhearing him, Mike answered his question. "I have heard that it's about thirty feet to the bottom. But that's only to the part that you can see. The bottom you are looking at slants down and sideways and ends up in a big cave. And from there, on to another cave and on down for more than two hundred feet to even more caves."

Mike continued. "Divers from the San Marcos Area Recovery Team made a videotape of the tunnel and cave bottom. We'll go look at that in the education center sometime."

Luis continued staring at the well; he could not take his eyes off the deep hole just inches from his feet. "What a strange place," Luis said to nobody in particular. "It looks like something from another world." He inched closer to the edge of the opening.

Without any warning an irrational feeling of foreboding overtook Luis. A wave of fear washed over him. He was unable to move, his body frozen into place at the rim of the well. His heart beat rapidly and his chest felt tight, but Luis could not take his eyes off the deep clear shaft before him.

The walls of the well bulged with coral-like boulders. They seemed to move in and out like giant lungs. Algae clung to the sides and undulated in a ghostly manner. Sinister. That was the word that jumped into Luis's mind. Yes, there was something sinister and terribly frightening about the well. Luis felt that some force was compelling him, drawing him closer and closer to the opening. Any minute the invisible thing would pull him into the icy depths of the well. Finally, Luis was able to step back. He took another step backward, his fear easing somewhat as he distanced himself from the well.

"Hey, Luis," said Sarah as Luis stepped from the water. "You looked a little weird out there. Are you okay?"

"Oh, sure," answered Luis, unwilling to let the others know of the strange experience. "I'm fine. It's just that the water is so cold."

Luis didn't want to admit that even the cliff and the surrounding rocks now seemed menacing. Luis shuddered. *Get hold of yourself,* he thought. *This is stupid; it's just a hole in the ground and some rocks.*

"Okay, lunch is over. Let's explore," said Hannah. "Why don't we cross the creek and climb the cliff rocks? We can roam around and see what the well looks like from up there."

CHAPTER 6

The Scream

Mike gathered up the sandwich wrappings and stuffed them into his backpack. "We'll have to wade across."

"Brrr," said Luis, reluctant to stick his feet back into the icy water. "Oh, well, here goes."

Shoes and socks in hand, Sarah, Mike, and Hannah followed Luis into the water. Luis was careful to stay as far from the edge of the well as possible.

"Look," cried Sarah, as they neared the rocky cliff wall. "Somebody has built some steps here in this crevice."

"Great," said Hannah. "I wasn't exactly looking forward to scaling those rocks."

The four climbed the narrow stairway and soon were atop the cliff. "I don't know which way this place looks prettier," commented Hannah. "It's awesome from down there looking across at the cliff. But it's just as impressive to look down from up here."

Luis stared down at the well. Somehow from this height, it looked less frightening. Just an unusual and beautiful place out in the woods, he told himself.

"The education center is about a half-mile east of here," said Mike. "But today let's just wander around. If we go south, we should come to a small valley."

"I hate it when you tell us to go east or go south," complained Hannah. "In these woods, it all looks the same to me. Why don't you just say right or left? Then I would know which way to go!"

Mike laughed. "You sound just like Mom. She's always saying that to Dad. Guess it's a female thing," Mike teased. "Next time I'll bring a compass. That will help us all get our bearings. Hey, that could be one of our projects. We could draw a map of the area."

"Good idea," agreed Sarah.

"Let's cut over this way and see if we can find the valley," said Mike. "Oh, and keep your eyes peeled for arrowheads. But if you find one, leave it where it is and we'll mark the spot some way. That's part of the deal we've worked out, not to move any artifacts we find."

"Artifacts from American Indians?" asked Sarah. "Do you know what tribe?"

"I was told at the education center that they were Tonkawas," answered Mike. "I read somewhere that the Tonkawas were known for their friendliness. That's about all I remember. Except for what Grandpa told us about Gray Wolf."

"Who was Gray Wolf?" asked Luis.

Mike looked at Hannah and grinned. "Oh, he's just a ghost who lives around here," he said airily.

Sarah paled. "What do you mean a *ghost*? A *ghost* lives here? In these woods?"

"Actually," said Mike, "we don't know where he lives, but we know where he shows up, don't we, Hannah?"

"Yes," said Hannah. "And our Great Uncle Ezra saw him. And so have other people, on a big rock down by the creek."

"Well, I hope I don't see him," Sarah said emphatically.

Hannah, Luis, and Sarah trudged behind Mike through the underbrush. "Mike," said Sarah, "I sure hope you know where you are going. I'm completely lost."

"I've got a pretty good idea," answered Mike. "I've been here before, but I entered the property from another road. That was a while back, though, and things don't look the same now."

"If you are trying to give us confidence in your orienteering ability, it's not working," joked Luis. "I think you need—"

Luis never finished his sentence. The air was filled with an unearthly, bone-chilling cry like nothing the four friends had ever heard before. Then silence. No birds sang, there was no rustling of squirrels in the brush, nothing. Just eerie silence.

"What... what was that?" asked Sarah in a hushed voice. "One of your friendly American Indians?" she asked shakily.

"Well, I don't exactly know," answered Mike. "But since it is winter and the days are short, I think we ought to head for home."

Mike was fighting hard to keep his alarm from showing. He couldn't let the others see that he was just as scared as they were.

The four of them made their way back toward the rock cliff, half expecting some loathsome creature from another world to step out to meet them. Grateful to see the cliff at last, they made their way down the steps of the rock face and across the stream to their bikes.

"I think whatever made that noise was just trying to tell us it's time to leave," joked Mike as he got on his bike. "Mr. Bartle warned me that we had to be out of here well before dusk because that is when he locks the gate. And I for one don't want to spend the night here."

"I'll second that," laughed Hannah nervously as she rode toward the gate.

"I hope we don't have nightmares tonight," added Sarah.

Luis was quiet as he followed the others on his bike. He couldn't throw off the feeling that something or someone was watching them... something or someone whose intentions were not good.

CHAPTER 7

Computer Animal Hunt

Several days later Hannah, Luis, and Sarah stood behind Mike as he worked at his computer. "Look what I found," said Mike as he brought up a wildlife site on the screen. "This may be what scared us."

A picture of a bobcat formed on the screen. Beside it was a map of the counties in Texas in which bobcats had been seen.

"Well, what do you know," exclaimed Luis with surprise. "Those cats are in every single county in the state. But are you sure a bobcat makes a noise like that? The noise we heard sounded almost like... like... Well, I can't describe it except that it was terrifying."

"I'm not sure about the sound," replied Mike. "I did find that the Texas mountain lion's mating call is described as a blood-curdling scream. So maybe it could even be a mountain lion."

Mike continued to search the Internet. "Look," he exclaimed excitedly, "here is a site with the sounds of the bobcat and mountain lion. Let's see if they sound like what we heard."

The four waited for the site to load. Suddenly, the computer speakers exploded with an animal's roaring scream.

"That's the mountain lion," said Mike. "Here's the bobcat." Another roar filled the room.

"Wow," exclaimed Hannah with a shudder. "As I remember, it sounded more like the first animal, the mountain lion. It's pretty scary to imagine that a mountain lion could have been out there. We'll have to be very careful when we go back."

Mike was still reading information from the web site. "It says here that on the travel routes of the mountain lions you can find *scrapes*."

"Scrapes?" asked Sarah. "What are they?"

"Well, it seems to be a way the male lion marks his territory. He scrapes together little piles of leaves and grasses and urinates on them. You usually find them along rimrocks and ridges where he's been."

Hannah said, "Mike, tell them what the game warden said."

"Oh, yeah," said Mike. "The other day in the hardware store, I saw a game warden and asked him if he ever saw any bobcats or mountain lions around here. He said he had seen both. What's interesting is that the bobcat stays fairly close to home, but the mountain lion sometimes travels in a ninety-mile radius from his home base."

"Wow," said Luis. "That's a big territory."

"Oh, and something else," added Mike, "he said the lions sometimes come all the way up here from Mexico looking for food, especially if there's a drought in Mexico."

"So should we be roaming around a place that's home to animals like that?" asked Sarah. "I'm not sure I want to tackle a science project that involves ferocious wild beasts."

"Aw, Sarah," said Mike. "That pit bull Mr. Andrews owns is probably ten times more dangerous than the mountain lion or the bobcat. The cats are nocturnal animals and not likely to mess with us since we don't plan to be around that place after dark."

"Also," Mike added, "the game warden said the cats are getting plenty of deer to eat right now. So don't worry about it, Sarah. Whatever that animal was, it probably was just passing through anyway."

Mike hoped it really was a mountain lion. The idea of any human making a sound like that was more frightening than any animal. And he hoped he was reassuring Sarah. At least he was making himself feel a little better.

— CHAPTER 8 —
The Stone Appears

Several weeks later, the four friends met at Luis's house. "Okay, now," said Mike, "let's check and be sure we have all our stuff. I have the compass and pencil and paper so we can begin work on our map. Hannah, is the tape measure in your backpack?" Hannah nodded.

Mike continued his checklist. "We all need to take responsibility for getting these supplies out to the well each time we go. Sarah, you've got the camera, right?"

"Yeah," said Sarah. "I just wish it were an underwater camera. Wouldn't it be great to drop it down the well and take pictures? But we can take some from the top of the well looking down and of course get some good shots of the area."

"Everybody have water?" asked Mike. They all nodded.

"I have lunch for all of us," said Sarah. "So let's hit the road!"

"Maybe we ought to pack some cat food for our wild friend in the woods," joked Luis. "You are all acting really cool with the idea of a mountain lion at Jacob's Well, but I confess, I am not looking forward to meeting up with that thing face to face."

The four went outside to their bikes. Hannah adjusted her backpack and asked Mike, "What's the plan for today?"

"There are several things we can work on today. One is to begin marking a path from the top of the cliff steps over to the valley. Later on we will mark a path from the valley up to the education center. Since the whole area is very rocky we can put a line of rocks to mark the way. Later we can define the path better."

Arriving at the clearing, they pushed their bikes into a thicket of small trees. "Everybody lock your bikes," Mike told his friends. "We may be getting more visitors out here as the weather warms."

Shoes and socks in hand, the four friends once again waded toward the cliff side of the well.

Luis glanced over at the well, telling himself softly, "It's just a well. It's just a well. Yeah, right. If it's just a well, why do I still have this spooky feeling?"

Aloud to the others he commented, "I thought the water would have warmed up some since the weather is a little warmer." Luis stepped out of the water. "But it is still the iciest water I ever had my feet in. Mr. Bartle says we can swim whenever we want to. I don't think I'm ready yet."

The sun-warmed rocks felt good to their bare feet. Sitting on the wide rock shelf, they pulled on their socks and shoes.

"Let's just walk to the valley and back," suggested Mike. "I think the path is fairly clear now, but let's make certain before we mark it."

The four walked from the cliff to the valley, then retraced their steps. "I think we are ready to begin marking the path," said Mike. "It might be best if we pick up rocks several yards off the path so it won't be so noticeable. And keep your eyes and ears open for our cat friend."

"Thanks a lot, Mike," said Sarah. "I was trying not to think about that mountain lion."

They found numerous chunks of limestone in assorted sizes and brought them to the path. "Hey, this is going to be really neat," said Hannah, lugging a stone to drop in line with others.

The friends worked quietly for an hour or so as their trail through the woods became more apparent.

Sarah picked up a fairly large stone and moved it to the path. Returning to the spot to brush some leaves over the bare place, she noticed what looked like a flat rock buried in the ground.

Sarah rubbed her fingers over the stone.

"Hey, guys," Sarah called, "come look at this. This rock has what looks like an s carved into it." The others gathered around Sarah, who was now scraping the area with a stick to expose more of the stone.

"Look," she said with excitement in her voice. "It looks like a gravestone or something." She continued removing the dirt and the others helped with sticks and bits of rock. More letters and then some numbers appeared on the face of the buried stone.

"Well, if that is a gravestone, the person sure had a strange name," commented Luis, as the letters on the flat stone were revealed.

"Herein lies the secret 50N, 20E, 14S," Luis read aloud. "That's it? What the heck does that mean?"

"The stone looks really old," said Sarah. "See how some of the letters and numbers are worn. And it looks like it has been covered for years and years. It's sure not an American Indian artifact. What is it?"

"Let's uncover the whole thing and see if we can pick it up," said Luis, digging around the edge of the

stone. "There must be something buried under it. Maybe it's gold or diamonds, or the loot from a robbery."

"Luis," said Hannah, "one of these days that wild imagination of yours is going to get you in trouble."

"Well, it could be a treasure. Who knows?" Luis answered with a shrug.

They all continued to dig. "I wish we had a spade," remarked Hannah. "This sure would go faster."

"We seem to have all the edges uncovered now," said Sarah, scraping deep around one edge. "Let's see if we can pick it up."

Sarah and Mike tugged at the edge of the rock, but it sat firm.

"We need to dig out all around it and see how deep it goes," said Luis. "Come on, let's keep digging around the edges." Each one worked at a side of the rock.

"Hey, I can feel the underneath part, so I think after just a little more digging we can move the thing," said Mike. His voice reflected his excitement. "All right, here we go. Everybody pull."

The rock began to move as they wrenched it loose from its burial place. They began to lift it, and at that moment they once again heard the eerie sound they had heard before. Was it really a mountain lion? Or was it some otherworldly creature which did not want them to remove the stone from its resting place?

"Omigosh!" breathed Sarah, frightened at the eerie sound. "I had convinced myself it was a mountain lion, but now I don't know. This is spooky and I'm scared. Something doesn't want us here. Maybe it's the ghost of Gray Wolf. Maybe we're invading his home or something."

Mike, trying hard to be the coolheaded leader, soothed Sarah. "Trust me, Sarah. It has to be a mountain lion. If we do come face to face with him, just stand up straight and still and look very tall."

"Ha, that's easy for you to say," replied Sarah with a shaky voice. "I could stand my tallest and probably not be any taller than the mountain lion."

"Think about it, Sarah," said Mike. "This time the sound came from much farther off, so we have nothing to worry about."

"But, Mike," asked Hannah uneasily, "do you really think we should keep doing this?"

"Let's not be a bunch of nervous nellies over this," Mike answered. "Come on, Luis, let's move the stone."

Luis and Mike set the stone aside. "Now we can see what's underneath. Dig, everybody," Mike commanded. He began scraping with his piece of limestone.

Soon the four had dug about six inches into the ground. "This is useless," said Sarah. "Let's replace the stone and cover it with leaves. Then let's come back with a spade."

Luis spoke thoughtfully. "I don't think there is anything here anyway."

"You're probably right," agreed Hannah.

Mike spoke up. "Okay, guys. Looks like we have another mystery. Sarah, why don't you get a picture of this stone and we'll see if we can figure it out. I'll copy what it says and we can work on it when we get home."

"This place gets weirder all the time," said Hannah, shaking her head. "First, we hear some crazy animal sounds, and now we find this rock. What next?"

"What next?" echoed Luis. "Who knows? But I'll bet there *will* be a 'next.' I just hope it's something simple and explainable."

CHAPTER 9

Digging the Stone

Several weeks later the four friends sat on the bank of the creek. "We've been coming out here for about six weeks and we're making progress. Now it's time to sit and enjoy," said Mike. "We've got most of the path to the valley marked now, and it's looking good. Next time we come, let's plan to swim. It's getting warm enough, and it's time we jumped into the well!"

Luis's heart lurched. Jump into the well? He had almost convinced himself the well was just an interesting hole in the ground, but he wasn't sure he was ready to swim around in that spooky-looking pit. It certainly was not your typical old swimming hole!

They pulled their lunches from their backpacks and began to eat.

"Mike," said Sarah, "school has kept us really busy lately and we haven't had a chance to talk about the stone. I haven't come up with a thing. Anybody else have any ideas?"

"I've thought about it some," said Luis. "It must be directions. N could be north, E could be east, and S, south. If that's right, then we just measure off fifty..." He stopped. "Fifty what?" he asked. "Feet, yards, paces, what? And what kind of a secret could anybody have out here anyway?"

"Tell you what," suggested Hannah. "Let's take the spade and dig deeper under the rock and see if we find anything. And what's wrong with doing it right now?" she urged.

Spade in hand, Mike led the way across the creek and down the trail to the hidden stone. He brushed away the leaves hiding the stone, and he and Luis lifted the stone aside.

"I'll dig awhile," said Mike, "and then somebody else can have a turn. That means you women, too. That way if we do find a treasure, we can all say we dug it up."

"My brother, the optimist," said Hannah. "You're getting as bad as Luis!"

An hour later, everybody had taken several turns digging into the rocky ground until it was too difficult to dig anymore. "I think we have hit bedrock," said Sarah. "I'm ready to give up."

"Me, too," said Luis. "There's nothing here. Let's fill in the hole and cover the stone again with brush. We'll just have to try something else."

"Since there was nothing under the stone," said Sarah, "then we had better think about using the directions like Luis suggested."

"It's getting late," warned Mike. "I think we had better set out for home. We can come back out again soon. Saturday okay with everybody?"

CHAPTER 10
Measuring a Mystery

Saturday morning found the four students once again on the path to the mysterious stone. The sun shone through the live oaks, filling the area with a moving pattern of sun and shadow.

"I feel good about today," said Sarah. "Maybe today is treasure day."

"The only way we can find out anything is to start measuring," said Hannah. "Why don't we start with feet and see where we end up?"

"Sounds logical to me," agreed Mike. "Let's go!"

They made their way to the buried stone, which they now kept covered with leaves and marked with a triangular piece of limestone Sarah had found.

Mike held the compass in his hand. "Okay, I'm ready. Luis, I'll spot you in the right direction and the girls can measure with the tape. It may get tricky if trees are in the way, but here goes."

Mike stuck his arm out to point north, and Luis walked through the underbrush in the direction Mike was pointing. Sarah held one end of the tape while Hannah pulled the other toward Luis.

"Got it," called Hannah. "That's fifty feet, the end of my tape measure." She marked the place with a scrap of white cloth held down by a rock. "Now we go east for twenty feet."

Mike moved to the cloth marker and turned to face east. Again, Hannah stretched the tape toward Luis, who stood directly east of Mike.

"Okay," she called out. "That's twenty feet east. Now for the fourteen feet south."

Once more they positioned themselves to measure the fourteen feet south. "All right," called Hannah. "This is the place. Bring the spade and let's start digging."

Almost two hours later, the friends had dug a sizable hole, but with no evidence of anything ever having been buried there.

"Looks like we bombed out again," sighed Sarah. "I'm tired, I'm discouraged, and it's time to go home. I am ready to give up on the whole thing. We are just wasting our time and energy, digging stupid holes all over this place."

"Part of me agrees with you," said Mike thoughtfully, "but another part says we should at least give it a try using yards instead of feet. But that can wait until another time. Let's head home."

They started back to the path. As they worked their way through the underbrush, Hannah shouted, "Wait! Everybody stop. Come over here and see what I found."

The others hurried to her side.

"Look," Hannah pointed with her toe. "Isn't that an arrowhead?"

"Yeah, it sure is," said Mike. "Wow, good job, Hannah."

Hannah started to pick up the flint point lying beside her toe. "Let's take it with us."

"No, don't pick it up," cautioned Mike. "Leave it where it is."

"Why?" teased Luis. "Are you afraid Gray Wolf's ghost will be mad at you?"

"It's not that," Mike said, giving his friend a poke in the ribs. "It's just that I promised David and Mr. Bartle we would leave any artifacts where we found them. We can mark the spot, though, so we can come back and look at it again."

"Let's put this big smooth stone over it," suggested Sarah.

"And here's a really funny-looking piece of tree

limb we can use," said Sarah. "It will help us recognize the spot easily."

Hannah carefully placed the bit of tree limb over the rock. "There," she said. "I think we can find this place again."

Mike led the way as they trudged tiredly back to retrieve their bikes from the thicket and head out the gate to home, a hot dinner, and a welcome shower.

CHAPTER 11
The Picture

"Okay, gang. One more time and that's it," Mike stated as the group arrived at Jacob's Well. "We'll measure in yards this time and then that's that! No more digging and hoping for buried treasure." He added, "We'll have to do the measuring quickly. We came out here later than usual, and we don't want to get locked in. But first I want to show you something."

Mike pulled a piece of paper from his backpack. "I printed this off a Jacob's Well site on the Internet. It's a picture of a diver down in the well. The white figure to the right is the body of another diver who died during a dive. Something went wrong. I think he was really deep, maybe in the third or fourth cave down."

Mike handed the picture to the others to look at. "Gosh," said Sarah, "that's the saddest thing I ever saw. Think how awful that must have been for him to die like that."

Sarah passed the picture to Hannah. Hannah shuddered at the thought of such a death. "That's a frightening picture," she said as she passed it on to Luis.

Luis took the picture and stared at it.

"Eight divers have died in Jacob's Well," Mike continued. "Some sources say nine or even more." Mike paused thoughtfully.

"Explain something to me," said Luis. "You said that in this last exploration the divers went really deep. How come nobody has explored that deep in the well before now?"

"Good point," said Mike. "Do you remember when we had that big flood a couple of years ago? A bunch of town houses were washed away. And re-member how the flood waters came over the low-water bridge in our subdivision? Even big slabs of the asphalt paving were washed off into the meadow."

"Yeah, I remember," said Hannah. "That was a powerful flood. We walked down to the creek after-wards to watch stuff float by. It was exciting."

"Well," Mike went on with his story. "That same flood caused some changes deep down in the caves. It seems that over the years, gravel had washed into the caves and partially blocked the openings. Then a couple of years ago, diving experts were called in to do some mapping of the caves. This time when the divers got down really deep, they found that floods had washed away a lot of the gravel. The openings were bigger and they were able to get a good look into the fourth cave, about 120 feet down."

Luis's eyes were still locked on the white figure in the picture. He again felt fear, the same fear he felt when he first looked down the chasm that is the well. But this time he would have described his feeling as sheer terror.

"I *knew* it," Luis burst out. "I knew there was something terrible and sinister about that well. This could happen to us if we swim in the well."

"Wait a minute, Luis," said Mike calmly. "These guys were divers, and I don't mean just diving in like somebody would in a swimming pool, for fun. They were exploring the cave and they were down very deep, probably too deep. Nobody knows what happened. But *we* are not about to do that," Mike continued. "All we will ever do is just swim around at the top."

Luis looked again at the eerie picture of the white figure suspended, floating in the watery space down deep in Jacob's Well.

"I don't care what you say, this is just plain spooky," said Luis, handing the picture back to Mike. "Let's hurry up and take those last measurements." Luis was anxious to get that picture out of his mind although he didn't think he could ever forget it, ever erase it from his memory.

Back once again at the mysterious stone, the group organized to mark off the space, this time fifty yards to the north.

"You realize," said Hannah, "that this is going to be 150 feet. That's a pretty good distance north."

"Not really," said Mike. "The lot our house is on is 150 feet deep. So just think about this as the same distance as from the street to our back fence."

Sarah stretched the tape out toward the north. "Here's fifty feet," she called. "Hannah, bring your end of the tape up here where I am standing and we'll measure our next fifty feet."

Hannah moved through the brush to Sarah. "The underbrush is thicker in here. It's hard to see what is up ahead."

"You're right," said Mike, stepping out ahead of Sarah. "Luis and I will trample some of this stuff down and make it easier for you." The boys moved in front of Sarah as she pulled out the tape once more.

"Just follow me," said Mike. "I'm keeping my eye on the compass so we'll be sure to go directly north."

Mike, Luis, and Sarah pushed through the underbrush at a slow pace. "Whoa," said Mike. "We have a problem. There's a fence here with a "*No trespassing*" sign on it. Frankly, I don't think we should go any farther anyway. Why wouldn't whoever carved that stone just use feet? After all, yards convert to feet and nobody measures acreage in yards, anyway."

"Yeah, you're right, Mike," agreed Luis. They turned to retrace their steps to Hannah.

"Lost cause, Hannah," said Mike. "We were stopped by a fence."

"Somebody worked hard to engrave that message on the stone," mused Sarah, as they made their way back to the path. "It has to mean something."

"I think you're right," agreed Hannah. "We just haven't figured it out yet.

"Come on, guys," called Mike. "We had better hurry. It won't be long until the sun sets. I haven't been paying much attention to the time. It's later than I thought."

"You're right," said Sarah. "Look how low the sun is. And the woods are even beginning to get dark. I don't like this. Let's hurry. Please."

Mike quickened his steps, but the brush was

heavy and thick. Long grasses whipped at their legs. Tangled masses of weeds seemed to snatch at them, trying to grasp them and hold them captive in the darkening woods.

"There's the path," Mike called back to his friends. "It will be easy going now."

They made their way more quickly and soon were climbing down the steep steps of the cliff.

Back across the creek once more, the four friends got on their bikes and rode toward the gate.

"Uh-oh," said Luis, as they neared the gate. "We have a problem, a definite problem."

"I see what you mean," said Mike. "We, my friends, are locked in. And I mean locked in for the night."

CHAPTER 12
Locked In

"This is sure not the way I wanted things to turn out today," said Mike as they sat together beside the creek. "I feel like it's my fault. I should have been watching the time more carefully."

"Mike, don't blame yourself," said Hannah. "We all have watches and we know how to tell time. We were just careless, but we'll make the best of it. Besides, you told Mom where we were going, so somebody will come looking for us."

"What do you mean, I told Mom? I thought you told Mom," said Mike.

"No, I didn't," said Hannah. "You mean nobody knows where we are?" Hannah swallowed hard, almost in tears.

Sarah spoke up. "I didn't tell anybody at my house where I would be. Since there's only Mom and she's at work, I told her to call your parents whenever she wanted to find me."

"Same here," said Luis. "I told my parents to just check with yours, because your folks always know where we are."

"Well, I am sure our parents will come looking for us. They'll figure out where we are, so let's not worry about it right now." Mike said this reassuringly, but he did not look forward to spending the night at the well.

As the sun set behind them, the group made their plans for the night. "We can use our backpacks for pillows and sleep out here by the creek," Sarah said.

"We have plenty of clean drinking water, anyway," joked Hannah, looking over at the well.

"And I've got a surprise for you," said Sarah. "Look what I have in my backpack." She pulled out a big box of cheese crackers. "And that's not all," she added triumphantly. "I always keep a stash of my favorite candy bars, just in case."

"You sure came prepared!" Hannah said. "Do you always keep that much food in your packpack?"

"Well, you never know when you might need a snack," answered Sarah.

"Does anybody have a flashlight?" asked Luis. "I don't think there will be much of a moon tonight."

"Yeah," answered Hannah. "Mike and I always carry flashlights in case we are caught out after dark. And I even have extra batteries."

"Well," said Luis, "we sure picked a good pair to be marooned with, didn't we, Sarah?"

"You're right," replied Sarah. "But if we have flashlights, couldn't we find our way to the education center? Wouldn't we be safer there?" she asked uneasily.

"There are a couple of problems with that," answered Mike. "One is that even with flashlights we could easily lose our way in these woods. The second problem is that even if we made it to the education center, it would be locked and nobody would be there. The gate at the center is locked at night, too. So we are better off staying right here."

"Yeah, I guess you're right," sighed Sarah.

Although everyone was making an effort to keep the atmosphere light, they were all uneasy about spending the whole night at the well. But there was nothing to do but make the best of a bad situation.

Sarah opened the box of crackers and passed it around. "Anybody got a story to tell?" she asked. "We've got no TV, no books to read. Seems like a good time for stories."

"As a matter of fact," said Mike, "I have a story I have been meaning to tell you all. It's about the well. You remember hearing about the divers who died in the well? The eight divers who have died down there over the years?"

Mike continued. "One of those divers spent the night right here with two of his good friends and fellow divers. They had tents and camping equipment with them and, unlike us, planned to spend the night here.

"They built a campfire and this one guy, I'll call him Zack, had brought his guitar with him. So they all sat around the campfire and Zack played his guitar and sang lots of good old favorite western songs. Sometimes the others sang along with him, but mostly it was just Zack singing and playing his guitar. It was a good night with good camp food, good comradeship, and good music.

"They all slept well, and the next morning they got into their diving gear and plunged into the well. Only thing is, Zack never made it out. Had a problem with his tank and died in the well."

Sarah shivered. "That is scary, Mike. Did you have to tell us this now at this particular time when we are stuck out here in this spooky place? Good gosh!"

"That's not all, Sarah," said Mike. "Legend has it that Zack left his guitar on the rock ledge across the creek and that his ghost comes back and plays the guitar. People around here swear they have heard his guitar music in these woods."

Hannah punched her brother. "Mike, you are downright mean to tell us such a story. There is probably not a word of truth in it."

Mike laughed. "Ooh, my children, do not be so sure. Listen carefully for the music of the guitar on this dark and creepy night."

"Mike, I'm going to bonk you with a rock if you don't shut up," said Sarah, teasingly, but with a note of anger in her voice.

Luis had sat quietly, listening attentively to Mike's story. In his mind's eye, he could see clearly the picture of the dead diver, a picture he wished he could forget. Of course, he didn't believe any ghost was hanging around waiting to play a guitar.

"Thank goodness, it's not a rainy night," said Sarah. They all knew what she meant. They had not forgotten about the ghost of Gray Wolf.

By now, the sun was gone and the darkness was complete. Clouds covered whatever moon there might have been. The few stars they could see did little to brighten the night but at least it was not the kind of weather that brought Gray Wolf from his ghostly hiding place.

Sarah shivered. "This is creepy. I wish I were home."

The kids sat quietly for a few minutes. "Listen to those frogs and crickets," remarked Luis, attempting to get his mind off Mike's story of the diver. "It's a regular chorus. That's really a nice summertime kind of sound." He was trying hard to convince himself that this was just an ordinary camping trip, but he was not being very successful.

Then an unpleasant thought crossed Luis's mind. He remembered Mike saying that the mountain lion was a nocturnal animal, doing his roaming and hunting at night.

"Oh boy, Mike," Luis said, "all we need now is for that mountain lion to come roaming around."

"Nah," said Mike. "We haven't heard him in a long time now. I am sure he's long gone from these parts."

"Thanks, Luis, for bringing up the mountain lion," said Hannah sarcastically. "I had forgotten about the lion. Well, here's to a good night's sleep, everybody," she said as she put on her sweater and laid her head on her backpack. "I am going to do my best to get at least a little sleep."

— CHAPTER 13 —
Ghostly Music

As uncomfortable as sleeping on the ground was, Hannah, Mike, and Sarah soon fell asleep. Only Luis was awake, listening to the night sounds. Several times he heard the padding footsteps of deer. At least he hoped they were deer, since deer were known to be plentiful in the area.

Mostly, however, Luis was thinking about the story of the diver and his guitar.

Finally, Luis's eyelids grew heavy and he began to drift off to sleep. His body relaxed and he was in that dreamy state between being awake and asleep when he heard another sound mingling with that of the night creatures.

His mind, suddenly alert, told him it couldn't be. But there it was, the distant sound of a guitar. Only a suggestion at first, it became stronger as though the guitarist were closing the distance between him and the music.

Luis sat up. "I'm dreaming," he muttered. "This can't be happening."

But the music continued. "Hey, you guys," he said in a loud whisper. "Wake up."

Sarah awoke first. "What is it, Luis?" she asked sleepily.

"Just listen," said Luis softly.

"Oh, no," said Sarah, her voice catching with fear. "It's guitar music. It's Zack's ghost!"

"Of course it's not the ghost," declared Luis. "There's no such thing as ghosts. You know it and I know it."

"Then, Mr. Luis, you just tell me who or what is walking around in these woods in the dark of night playing on a guitar." There was a note of panic in Sarah's voice.

Mike and Hannah were awakened by their friends' voices. "What's going on?" asked Mike, sitting up and stretching.

"Listen," said Sarah.

"Good gosh," exclaimed Hannah, suddenly wide awake. "Do you hear the same thing I hear, a guitar?"

"Yes, we all hear it," said Sarah. "I tell you, guys, this is just about too much. Mountain lions, stones with mysterious messages, dead divers, all kinds of ghosts. I am out of here in the morning and I may never come back!"

The eerie strains of guitar music continued for another hour, sometimes fading, sometimes sounding as though the guitarist were just across the creek. Then the music stopped abruptly.

Mike, Hannah, Luis, and Sarah sat huddled together wishing dawn would hurry, but grateful that at least the music was finally gone.

One by one they nodded off.

"Wake up, you guys," shouted Mike. "The gate's open. Let's get out of here."

Several minutes later four tired friends were pedaling through the gate. They were about to begin the climb up the steep hill when a car crested the hill. Mike squinted through his glasses.

"Look, it's Sheriff Mitchell," shouted Mike.

The car descended the hill, then pulled up beside the students. The sheriff rolled down his window. "Where in the devil have you kids been?" he asked. "Your parents have been nearly crazy with worry. They've had the whole town looking for you."

"We thought our parents would figure out where we were and come looking for us," answered Mike.

"But nobody ever came, so we just stayed at the well until Mr. Bartle unlocked the gate this morning."

Sheriff Mitchell looked thoughtful. "Well, they did figure you were probably out here, so we called Mr. Bartle. He said he checked the place before he locked up and you weren't here and he didn't see your bikes."

"We must have still been in the woods," said Luis. "And we always hide our bikes. Guess hiding our bikes is not such a good idea after all."

"You kids ride on home," said the sheriff. "I'll call your folks and tell them you're on your way. They'll sure be glad to know you're safe."

──CHAPTER 14──
Wonder Cave

Two weeks later Mike, Hannah, Sarah, and Luis were working together on an experiment in the science lab at school. Mike lined up the rock samples on the lab table as they prepared to test them for hardness.

"Free, free! Free at last!" Luis suddenly burst forth happily.

"Yeah," said Hannah, rubbing a piece of talc between her fingers. "It's been a long two weeks. Being grounded is no fun. Mike and I weren't even allowed to go anywhere on our bikes."

Sarah chimed in. "Well, at least we all had the same punishment. And you have to admit, we did goof by not letting our parents know where we had gone when we got stuck out at the well. Now I have to leave a note on the kitchen counter if I even go next door for a minute."

"Me, too," said Luis. "What a pain."

"Now that we are allowed to go somewhere again, we need to make plans," said Mike.

"I know nobody is ready to go back out to the well anytime soon," said Hannah, "but we have to keep working on our report. How about concentrating for a while on the other part of our cave report, caves that are underground but not underwater?"

"I think I know what you have in mind," said Mike. "A day at Wonder World Park in San Marcos. Just what we need."

"I'll ask Mom if she can take us this Saturday," said Sarah. "Can you guys all make it then?"

Mike, Luis, and Hannah nodded in agreement. "Sounds good to me," said Hannah.

Saturday morning found the four at the entrance to Wonder Cave. "You won't believe this," said Luis, as they bought tickets for the cave tour, "but I have lived in Wimberley six years and only fifteen miles from this place and I have never been here. We come to San Marcos at least once a week, but never have come to Wonder World."

"You'll like it," said Sarah. "I love this place, especially the cave."

"What's hard for me to believe is that all this part of Texas was once under the sea," said Hannah. "The cave itself was formed in an earthquake. It's on a fault line. In fact, I have read that it is the same fault line that runs through Jacob's Well."

"We talked about fault lines in our earth science class," said Luis. "But do you mean to tell me that we are living in an earthquake zone?"

"Not to worry, my friend," answered Mike. "It all happened millions of years ago." Mike paused, then added thoughtfully, "Of course, there was an earth-quake here about five years ago. We could have an-other one any minute, probably when we are in the deepest room," he teased.

"All right, Mike," said Sarah. "Enough of that. You know there hasn't been another earthquake here. Let's just enjoy the tour."

Mike and Luis swung open the double doors lead-ing to the entrance of the cave. "After you, ladies," Mike said, bowing as he and Luis held the doors open.

"Honestly, Mike, sometimes you embarrass me, acting like that," chided Hannah.

"Just being a gentleman," responded Mike with a grin.

Inside the doors stood a young man in a green T-shirt with "Wonder Cave" printed on it in large white letters. "Hi, my name is Gary and I'll be your guide for the tour," he informed the small group assembled for the tour of the cave.

Gary counted aloud. "Okay. There are ten of you. Just want to be sure that if we take ten people into the cave, we bring ten people out! Before we get into the cave, I want to caution you to stay on the walkway and be extremely careful. There are some very steep and rough places."

Mike glanced at two elderly people who were part of the group. He was familiar with the hazards of the cave and hoped these two people could make it up and down the jagged, steep rock path that lay ahead of them. Also there were low, head-crushing rocks overhead and the cave was adequately but not brightly lit. It was not an easy trek even for the young and agile.

Mike heard Gary saying, "Now follow me down these stairs and I will take you to the first room." The tour group followed along quietly, and entered the first room, stepping carefully.

"This is called the poker room," Gary told the group, "because the original owner of the cave brought his friends down here to play poker. It was cooler than the Texas heat outside, and," he added with a grin, "it got the men away from their wives, who didn't approve of gambling."

"I thought there would be those formations on the floor and ceiling, stalactites or stalagmites," Luis commented to Sarah. "I never remember which is which."

"Oh, there's a good trick for remembering the difference," said Hannah. "The word stalactite has a 'c' in the middle of it—think 'c' for ceiling. Stalagmite has a 'g' in the middle—think 'g' for ground. Trust me, you won't forget it now."

"That does help," said Luis. "Thanks. But why aren't there any in this cave?"

Mike answered. "The part of the cave we are in now and most of what we will see is called a dry cave. There's nothing dripping down to form the stalactites and stalagmites. But there is a room the owners call the Crystal Palace," Mike continued, "because it does have stalactites and stalagmites. We don't get to see that room and some of the other rooms because we would need hard hats, rope, flashlights, and other cave gear."

"I wish we could see that Crystal Palace room," said Hannah. "Just the name makes it sound like it would be the best part of the cave."

Mike continued. "There is only one wet place we will see where water drips constantly. But there are just a few tiny stalactites there. You'll see those when we get to what they call the flowstone in the next room."

Gary guided them down steep stairs. He pointed out the different layers of rock. "Look up at the big boulder above and behind you. You will see hundreds of marine fossil fragments embedded in it. Look carefully and you will see what looks like gold in the rock. That is iron pyrite, sometimes called fool's gold."

"Wow," exclaimed Sarah. "It does look like gold. I'll bet lots of people have been fooled by that."

They continued to yet another room as Gary described the various features of the cave. He pointed out the different rock layers, rapidly repeating the many scientific names.

"Chert, calcite, dolomite, limestone. I'm getting confused," complained Hannah. "How in the world can we remember all this stuff so we can put it in our report?"

"Don't worry about it," answered Mike. "Everything Gary is telling us is on the Internet. We just look up Wonder Cave and there it is."

"Good," answered Hannah with relief. "Now I can enjoy the cave without having to remember every single word he is saying."

CHAPTER 15
In the Dark

Gary led them down more steep steps and into a room with rock benches. "Everybody please sit down. I am going to turn out the lights now, so that you can experience complete darkness."

"I am not going to like this part," said Sarah apprehensively. "I was afraid of the dark when I was little. I would imagine that a witch was under my bed. I could almost feel her bony hand creeping up the side of the bed to grab me. Even on the hottest nights I would sleep with the covers pulled all the way over my head so she couldn't get me."

Sarah was quiet a minute. "I don't think I have completely outgrown it. Hannah, sit close to me so I will know you are there."

The group settled themselves on the benches and Gary touched a light switch. The resulting darkness was so deep Hannah felt she could reach out and touch it.

"This is scary," Sarah said to Hannah as she grabbed for Hannah's hand. "I can't see anything at all."

"Don't worry, Sarah," said Hannah, squeezing Sarah's hand. "Gary won't keep the lights off for long. Just long enough for us to see what real darkness is. Even when we think it is totally dark at night, there is still light from the moon or an electric clock or whatever. It is interesting to see how dark it really can be."

"Hannah, I'm scared," Sarah whispered. "What if Gary sneaks out and leaves us in the dark? What if the electricity goes off? What if we get locked in down here? Or have another earthquake? I want to get out of here."

"It's all right, Sarah. We'll be fine. The lights will go on any minute. And we only have a few more rooms to see." Hannah tried to reassure Sarah. "We'll be out of here before you know it."

They blinked as the lights came on. It had been dark for only a minute or two, but Sarah was shaking. "I sure would hate to have to stay in that darkness for long," Sarah commented with relief. "It's too creepy for me."

"We are now approaching the lowest part of the cave," announced Gary. "This is where we will see the well. The well itself is man-made, but the water comes from a lake that lies under the cave. An endangered species—the blind salamander—lives in the lake."

"I have heard that if you stay in total darkness for two weeks, you will go blind," said Luis. "Guess that's what happened to the salamander."

Sarah shuddered. She took a deep breath. *There's nothing to be afraid of,* she told herself.

Mike threw some pennies in the wishing well. "Here's your wishing well, Luis. Make a wish, everybody."

Sarah was wishing hard. "I just want to see the sky again and soon," she wished.

Gary pointed to the ceiling above the well. "See the black marks here and here? A hundred years ago, explorers in the cave would lower a bucket on a pulley to the water below to get a drink. The soot from their candles left these marks. Of course, those explorers didn't have the walkway and steps we have today. It was much more dangerous for them down here than it is for us."

Gary continued. "Head up the stairs in the passageway in front of you and enter the last room." The group trooped up the rock steps and gathered in the last room.

"This is called the Fossil Room," said Gary.

79

"Look around and you will see why. Above you the ceiling is full of fossils, the remains of a reef-building clam. Notice the unusual curving shapes. Some are almost circular."

Hannah looked carefully at the strange designs the fossils formed in the rock. "This rock reminds me of the stone we found with the message carved in it," she mused.

"I think this is the most interesting part of the cave," said Mike. "The fossils here are so weird looking. Gary, what was the name of the sea that covered all this?"

"It was the Gulf of Mexico," replied Gary. "If you drive about 200 miles south to Corpus Christi, you can swim in that same sea today."

Sarah gazed at the formations around her. "I keep thinking about what you said, Hannah, about all this and even Jacob's Well once being under the sea. This cave would probably have looked like Jacob's Well does now. At least the caves deep down in the well would look this way."

"Yeah," agreed Luis. "Somehow seeing this makes the well less scary. I can understand why divers would want to explore the caves in the well."

CHAPTER 16
The Elevator

"Okay, everybody," called out Gary. "This is the end of the cave tour. The elevator at the end of the room will take you up to the observation tower. We can only take part of you at a time as there is a weight limit for the elevator."

Since several of the people on the tour had questions for Gary, Mike, Hannah, Sarah, and Luis walked over to the elevator.

"Hey, we're getting out of here without anything going wrong," Luis said to his friends.

"What do you mean?" asked Hannah.

"Well, we didn't hear any weird sounds, or find strange messages, or hear eerie guitar music, or anything. We didn't even hear anything about a resident cave ghost. Kind of nice for a change, wouldn't you say?"

As they reached the elevator, the door to the small cubicle opened and the four stepped in. A young man greeted them. "Hi, I'm Rudy. Guess you guys are ready for a ride to the observation tower."

"I sure am," answered Sarah. "I am ready for sky, sunshine, and no more cave for a while."

The young man smiled. "We'll have you up and out in no time. Meanwhile, enjoy the ride. As we go up, we will be traveling through rock that took over 100 million years to form. You will see several other illuminated caves both to the back and to the front of the elevator."

He pushed several of the odd-looking switches beside his hand. The elevator car rose slightly.

Sarah looked around at the elevator. It seemed to be not much more than a metal cage with a door and some switches. She asked uneasily. "How old is this elevator? Are you sure this thing is safe?"

"Of course it's safe," he answered. "I don't know how old it is, but I go up and down in it all day long without a problem." He corrected himself. "Well, almost without a problem. Once in a while there's a glitch."

He had no sooner gotten the words out of his mouth than the small cage jerked to a halt. "Oops, this must be one of the glitches," Rudy said with a giggle. "Hang in with me for a few minutes and we'll get it started again."

Rudy flipped a row of switches, but nothing happened. He pushed on every control in the elevator, but still nothing happened.

Sarah laughed nervously. "Well, at least we are not in the dark."

Rudy continued to flip switches, but the little cage didn't move. He moved all the switches once more and the elevator jerked downward a few inches and stopped once again.

"Please, I want to get out of this thing," said Sarah, her voice rising in panic. "Please hurry and get us out."

Rudy answered, "Okay, I think I can get the door open. We should be back close to where we started, so I'll let you out if the door will open."

As he spoke, he pushed on the door and it creaked open. Sarah rushed through the opening and her friends followed. "Thank goodness we are out of that scary elevator," she said. "But what do we do now? There is nobody here. Where did the others go?"

Rudy spoke up. "Gary probably decided to take them back the way they came in. I guess they gave up when the elevator wouldn't work right. Tell you what. You wait right over there on those rock benches and I'll keep working with this elevator. When I get to ground level, I'll tell Gary to come back and get you and take you back through the cave to the entrance. You are the last tour for the day so if Gary's not available, I promise I will send somebody for you."

He closed the door to the elevator, and in a few minutes the four friends could hear it rising.

"Good," said Mike. "That problem is solved and we will be out of here soon. Sarah, to tell you the truth, I am glad to be out of that elevator myself. I am a little claustrophobic and elevators give me the creeps."

"Let's start walking back through the cave to meet Gary or whoever comes to lead us out," suggested Mike. "I don't think we will have a problem finding our way. Then we will be that much closer to getting out of here."

"Sounds good to me," said Hannah. "I am ready to get out of the cave and eat something. I am really hungry."

Mike led them as they retraced their steps. When they reached the wishing well, Mike stopped. "Let's stop here a minute and rest. In fact, this might be a good place to wait for Gary."

"Suits me," said Luis as he sat on a rock ledge. "Hey, Gary, come get us," he yelled, but there was no answer. He began to have a feeling their cave adventure was not going to be so trouble-free after all.

As they settled themselves on the hard rock seats, Sarah asked nervously, "Are there any bats in this cave?"

Hannah answered, "I heard somebody else on the tour ask that. Gary said there are no bats in here because there are no openings to the outside."

"Well, that's a relief," said Sarah. "Or maybe it isn't," she corrected herself. "If there is no way for bats to get in, then there's no other way for us to get out." A shadow of fear crept into her mind.

Sarah paused, then said, "I would suggest somebody tell a story to pass the time, but last time I did that Mike came up with all that scary stuff about the diver."

"Wonder why they keep the lights so dim in here," mused Hannah. "I guess it is supposed to add to the spooky atmosphere or something."

"I don't want to think about anything being spooky right now," said Sarah. "Let's change the subject. Luis, did you ever visit any caves when you lived in Mexico?"

"I heard a lot about the underwater caves in the Yucatan area," answered Luis, "but we never went there. I did visit one cave, though. It was nothing like this one. It was one stinky place!" Luis wrinkled his nose at the memory.

"There were sulphur springs inside the cave and they made the whole place smell like rotten eggs. It did have stalactites, though. I remember the guide calling them *snottites*. I thought that was an odd name. I didn't know whether it was Spanish or English, but now that I speak English, I think the name is even weirder!"

Sarah and Hannah giggled at the idea of dripping cave stones being called *snottites*. "Maybe we can put that in our report," said Hannah. "Our classmates would love it!"

— CHAPTER 17 —
Deep Darkness

"I wish Gary would hurry up and come get us," said Hannah. "There has been plenty of time for Rudy to send somebody for us."

"Unless there is still a problem with the elevator," said Mike. "Wonder if it was an electrical problem."

He had no sooner spoken than the lights flickered, dimmed, then brightened again. "I guess it *is* an electrical problem," he said, laughing.

The lights flickered once more, then went out, leaving the four friends in absolute and total darkness.

Sarah gave a frightened scream, then began to cry, sobbing softly. "I'm sorry to be such a sissy," she said between shuddering sobs.

Hannah said, "This would give anybody the creeps, Sarah. Just try to imagine it with the lights on— the well is in front of us, there are no bats or animals in here, we are safe and protected in here even if it is dark. Just think, if there is a thunderstorm outside, we don't have to worry about being hit by lightning!"

Sarah laughed through her crying. "Well, I guess there is something good about being trapped in a cave in total darkness. But I think I would rather be out in the storm."

Hannah asked Mike, "Don't you have a flashlight with you? You always go everywhere so well prepared."

"Not this time, I'm sorry to say. You remember we agreed that it wouldn't make sense to try to wear our backpacks through all these narrow and rough passages. So I never thought to put a flashlight in my pocket. Wish I had!"

"Maybe," said Luis, "we could feel our way out of the cave in the dark. No, no, forget that. We would bash our heads in on the rocks. We will just have to sit here and wait."

"One good thing," said Sarah. "My mom was going to meet us outside the gift shop at five o'clock. I don't know what time it is now, but Rudy said we were the last tour. If the gift shop closes and we aren't there, my mom will have everybody within five miles looking for us."

"You are right, Sarah. At least somebody knows where we are this time," said Mike.

"Well, to pass the time," said Luis, "I have a story. And don't worry, it's not a scary one. I don't know if it's true or not, but a book I just finished reading told about caves and tunnels below the city of Jerusalem. There was a treasure..."

Sarah interrupted. "There you go again, Luis, dreaming about treasure."

"Now just let me finish, Sarah. There was a treasure hidden in a secret room in the winding passages. The treasure was not gold or silver or jewels, but ancient manuscripts preserved for thousands of years. Many wars have been fought over Jerusalem, and because over the years the rabbis wanted to keep the manuscripts secret, only a few people knew about them.

"One of these rabbis decided it was time to show the scrolls to a younger man, so he took the young man down into the passages. The tunnel was so secret that they couldn't take the chance of even candlelight showing through anywhere to the outside. The rabbi blew out the candles and the two of them were in complete darkness just like we are. Now here's the good part.

"The rabbi told the young man to run his fingers across the ceiling. There he would feel a groove. 'Put your finger in the groove,' the rabbi told the young man, 'and keep it there as we crawl along.'

"The young man did as he was told as they crawled through the tunnel. The tunnel wound this way and that. Sometimes it made sharp turns or went off to the left or to the right. He always kept his finger in the groove on the tunnel ceiling over his head. Sure enough, the young man and the rabbi soon entered the room where the sacred scrolls were kept." He paused before asking, "So how do you like that story, Sarah?"

"That is really neat, Luis. I sure wish we had some grooves to follow in this cave. Or some of the old-timers' candles would be even better."

"Did you hear something?" Mike whispered. "I thought I heard a voice."

They all grew quiet and strained to listen for a sound. There was only silence, made even deeper by the darkness.

"I guess I imagined it," said Mike. "But somebody ought to be looking for us by now."

Hannah sighed loudly. "Let's sing," she suggested.

"Ha," snorted Luis. "It's bad enough being in the dark, trapped in a cave way underground. No way I am going to punish you guys with my off-key voice! You have enough problems."

The others laughed.

Hannah asked Sarah, "Are you okay?"

"Yes, I am sort of getting used to it. And you know, it makes you think about all the good things we have and how lucky we all are. Having good eyesight is really a blessing, isn't it?"

"You'd better believe it," said Mike. "I thought it was a pain to have to wear glasses, but that's nothing compared to this!"

CHAPTER 18
Finally Rescued

"Shhh," cautioned Luis. "I am pretty sure I heard somebody."

Once again they strained to hear a sound, then very faintly, a voice sounded in the far-away end of the cave.

"Hey, we're here," they all began to yell at once. "We're here by the well."

The four listened once more. "I'm on my way," they heard someone calling in the distance.

"It's Gary. Hooray! We'll be out soon," said Mike, his voice filled with relief.

Soon they saw a pinpoint of wavering light. The light grew closer and they could see that it was a flashlight. In another few moments, Gary was beside them.

"Wow," he said, "you guys must have been scared to death down here in the dark."

"Oh, not really," said Mike. "We just sat around and told stories. Nothing to it."

"What a liar," said Hannah. "You were scared and you know it!"

"I guess so," Mike confessed, "but Gary, we knew you would rescue us sooner or later. Tell us what happened to the lights."

Gary replied, "We aren't sure what happened, but apparently the lights went out all over town. Rudy finally managed to get the elevator running enough to get it to ground level just before everything went out. When he finally got the door opened and found me, he told me you four were still down here. So here I am. This flashlight will give us enough light to get us out as long as we go slowly and step carefully."

Gary led them back through the rocky passages and when they reached the poker room, they knew they were almost out of the dark cave.

"Up these stairs, through the gift shop, then out into the blinding sun. Cover your eyes as we leave because that sun will be a bit of a shock after the darkness."

Finally, the four friends emerged into the dazzling sunlight.

"Texas sun is hotter than heck," said Mike, "but it sure feels good to me right now."

"Yeah," said Sarah. "Boy, am I glad to be out of there. Luis, what was it you were saying about nothing going wrong in the cave?" she teased.

Sarah's mom was waiting in the minivan. "I hear you had a little adventure in the cave," she said. "You must be hungry after something that nerve-wracking, so let's find you some food before we make the drive back home."

In a few minutes they were all in a fast food restaurant carrying their trays laden with hamburgers and French fries. As the four friends settled into their seats, Luis asked the others, "Are you guys about ready to get back to work at the well?"

"I sure am," answered Mike. "And I'm ready to dive into the well, too. I want to see what it looks like under the water."

"Me, too," said Luis. "I'm curious to see if it looks anything like what we saw at Wonder Cave." Luis did not mention the fear that still gripped him sometimes when he thought about the well.

"You realize," said Hannah, "that we probably won't get more than six feet down if that much. Some underwater cave explorers we are! We'll hardly be under the surface."

"Grandpa said they used to hold big heavy rocks when they jumped in, trying to sink further down."

"Did it work?" asked Sarah.

"From what he said, not much," answered Mike.

"Well," said Luis, "even if we don't get very far down, we will get an idea of what a deeper dive would be like. Why don't we go out on Monday? Monday and Tuesday are teacher workdays and we have a holiday."

"Let's ride to the deli tomorrow, get some ice cream, and talk about our plans," suggested Hannah.

— CHAPTER 19 —
Downtown Wimberley

The Sunday afternoon sunshine warmed the four friends as they walked their bikes across the Cypress Creek bridge in the little village of Wimberley. They stopped on the bridge to look down at the water falling over the rocks on its way to join the nearby Blanco River.

"Interesting, isn't it," mused Sarah, "that all this water is coming down from Jacob's Well. There is something kind of poetic about that."

The friends stood silently for a while, mesmerized by the scene. Huge cypress trees hung over the creek and ducks swam above the small waterfall.

Luis asked, "Do you guys know anything about that old house up on the hill, the one by the Senior Citizens' Center?"

"Yeah," answered Mike. "That's the old Winters house. Way back, more than a hundred years ago,

96

William Winters moved his family to Texas from the mountains in Tennessee. They were living in San Marcos and he wanted to explore the higher country around here.

"So he and another fellow, William Moon, set out from San Marcos. They followed the Blanco River all the way up from San Marcos. Then they came to the place where this creek flows into the Blanco, not very far from where we're standing right now.

"They went up the creek about six miles and found Jacob's Well. They thought the whole creek with the big cypress trees and little waterfalls was as pretty as anything they ever saw. It reminded Mr. Winters of the mountains in Tennessee."

"When was that, Mike? Did you say a hundred years ago?" asked Sarah.

Mike answered. "It was sometime after 1850 since he wasn't in the 1850 census records."

"Then it could be almost 150 years ago," said Hannah. "Wow, and his house is still here."

"Well," answered Mike, "first he built kind of a rough house and then he built that stone one you see up on the hill. I've been in it. It is really interesting. Maybe we can all go inside and see it sometime."

Luis commented. "I would think this village

would be called Winters or Wintersville or something. Why is it called Wimberley?"

"Glad you asked," said Mike.

"You do love to spout off information, Mike," his sister teased.

"Well, he did ask," said Mike with a twinkle in his eye. "To be honest about it, I did a social studies report on Wimberley history or I wouldn't know all this stuff.

"Anyway, to answer your question, Luis, Mr. Winters had built a mill by this creek. It was an all-purpose mill. Believe it or not, it was a flour mill, gristmill, sawmill, sorghum mill, and a cotton gin, too!

"In 1874," Mike continued, "a fellow named Pleasant Wimberley bought the mill and the town was called Wimberley Mill. In 1880 the U.S. Post Office shortened the name to Wimberley."

"My gosh, Mike," said Hannah. "You never told me that. That's really interesting."

Slowly the four walked on across the small bridge and to the square which was downtown Wimberley. "I love coming here on Sundays," said Hannah. "On weekends the town is full of tourists and you can see some real characters."

"Like that old guy in the rocking chair over there," said Luis. He nodded in the direction of the

porch in front of the Old Mill Store. "He must think he's sitting right on his own front porch."

"Yeah," said Mike. "He's a local character, for sure. He just shows up in town sometimes and sits over there and plays his guitar like he owns the place. Where he lives is sort of a mystery. In fact, nobody seems to know his real name. Around here they just call him Wimberley Willie."

"Let's cross over to the deli and get some of that good old Blue Bell ice cream," said Sarah. "The deli has it in those crunchy waffle cones I like so much."

Soon the four were seated at an umbrella table outside the little sandwich shop and feasting on their ice cream.

"Tastes good on a hot day, doesn't it?" Sarah asked contentedly.

"Yeah," answered Luis. He was watching Wimberley Willie across the way. "You know how something will almost come into your mind, like the answer to a question, or like a good idea, or maybe a memory? But it doesn't quite make it to the front of your brain?"

The others stared at him. "Luis," asked Mike, "what in the world are you talking about? Sometimes you lose me completely!"

"I can't exactly explain it. It's just that I feel like

that when I look at Wimberley Willie. I get this feeling that he could be the answer to some question, but I don't know what the question is."

"And on that note, my friends," said Mike, standing up, "let us depart this place and wend our way back home."

Hannah gave her brother a playful kick. "Honestly, Mike, sometimes you sound like you are making a speech instead of just having a conversation!"

CHAPTER 20

Into the Well

Swim suits on under their shorts and T-shirts, the four friends rode through the Jacob's Well gate on Monday morning.

Finding a shady spot to leave their bikes, they sat down to cool off before going swimming.

"How do you feel about going into the well, Luis?" asked Sarah, remembering the look on his face when they first visited the well.

"Oh, I'm okay with it," answered Luis in what he hoped was a confident voice. "It's just a hole in a creek. And it's not like we are going down into the caves."

"Here we go then," said Hannah. Pulling off her shorts and shirt and putting them beside her shoes on the bank. Hannah waded over to the well.

"Yippee," she yelled, plunging into the well. She surfaced seconds later. "Hurry up. The water's great—cold as heck, but it feels good."

Sarah and Mike followed, jumping feet first into the well.

Luis stood at the edge of the well as the eerie feeling of danger crept into him once more. "It's just a hole in the ground, it's just a hole in the ground," recited Luis as he followed his friends into the water. He surfaced and swam to the edge of the well.

"What do you think, Luis?" asked Hannah. "How does it feel to actually be in the well?"

"Surprisingly, not as scary as it does to stand in the creek and look down," answered Luis. "I'm going to dive down and look around some."

Luis swam downward, wishing he had brought swim fins. He could feel the pressure of the water pushing him upward. Even so, he could see a little more of the well's sides.

Back at the surface, he called to the others, "It's great down there. Now I wish I could go deeper!" It was a relief to have overcome his fear of the well.

Then he remembered the picture of the body in the well and was glad to join his friends at the side of the creek. "I still find that well a little spooky," Luis admitted to Sarah as he placed his towel beside her on the rock ledge. "I sure wish I could forget some of that stuff Mike told us."

CHAPTER 21

The Videotape

Tuesday dawned gray and rainy. Mike was on the phone to Luis. "Yeah, it looks like our trip to the well is off, at least for this morning. Maybe the weather will clear by afternoon."

"Meanwhile, guess what!" Mike exclaimed, excitement in his voice. "I borrowed the videotape of the cave in Jacob's Well, the one the divers made. David let us borrow it."

"Great," said Luis. "I'll call Sarah, and the minute the rain slows down a little, we'll come over."

As soon as there was a letup in the rain, Luis headed for Mike's house on his bike. Sarah arrived at the same time, glad to have something to do during the rainy morning.

"Hi," said Hannah, opening the front door. "Come on in. Mike is getting the tape set up now. We are really lucky David let us use it. It belongs to the center, but since we have done so much work in the preserve, he's letting us use it."

"In the what?" asked Sarah.

"The Jacob's Well Preserve," answered Hannah. "Some people interested in protecting the water quality and the land have created a preserve. This group will make rules about use of the land and water and educate the community on how to take care of it. Since we are working to improve the area, we are part of this care group. Kind of neat, huh?"

"Yeah, I like that," answered Sarah. "It makes our science report all the more important. It's a good way to inform our classmates about how important it is to take care of Jacob's Well. But how exactly are people supposed to take care of the well?" asked Sarah.

"Well, one thing the Preserve group is worried about is the level of the water. More and more wells are being drilled around the area as more people move in and build homes. They all have to have water, and anything that pulls water out of the aquifer endangers the well."

"Yeah, and the conservation groups are urging people to collect rainwater," Hannah continued. "There are people in Wimberley who collect rainwater in a couple of really big tanks and they have never even had to drill a well."

"What about pollution in Jacob's Well?" asked Luis. "I know that's a big problem with all our lakes and rivers and even the oceans."

"You're right, Luis," said Hannah, "and that's a big worry with Cypress Creek and Jacob's Well, too. They worry about stuff like fertilizer and pesticides soaking through the ground into the water. And of course, sewage spills can be a big problem."

"That's really scary," said Sarah. "After all, that's the water we drink."

"Yeah," said Hannah, "and also there are probably some endangered species down there, too."

"We're ready," called Mike from the other room. The four settled down to watch the video. Mike started the tape.

Immediately, their attention was drawn to the eerie sounds on the tape. There were only two sounds and they repeated themselves over and over—one was what seemed to be the divers inhaling deep breaths from their air tanks and the other was the bubbling sound of the exhaled air. They were rhythmic, almost hypnotic sounds.

"The sounds are like something out of a horror movie," said Hannah quietly. "The creature from deep water space, or something."

"Creepy," agreed Luis.

The divers swam through water that was so clear it looked like air. "Wow, that's spectacular," said Luis. "That's the clearest water I ever saw. The divers look like they are floating through space."

"It's more beautiful down in the caves than I ever would have thought," said Hannah, awe in her voice. "I never realized the rocks down there would have so many colors. It's like another world."

The four friends watched as the divers went deeper and deeper. The lights carried by the divers played along the rocky walls. The divers were careful not to stir up any sediment from the bottom of the tunnel.

"Look at how careful they are not to touch the bottom," commented Mike. "I understand that if the divers get sloppy about that and the water gets full of silt, they can get disoriented and lost. They call it a silt-out.

"But even with all the risks, it is easy to see why somebody would want to explore down there," Mike continued. "It is really beautiful. But it's scary, too. I think I would have claustrophobia and feel trapped moving through such narrow spaces. Gives me the creeps to watch it. But at the same time I feel compelled to watch, almost like something is pulling me down into the cave with the divers."

"Yeah, I know what you mean," said Luis. The film was bringing back some of the fear he felt that first time he stood at the edge of the well. His mind's eye could see vividly the photograph of the bloated, white figure floating eerily in the water. Luis shuddered.

"I tried to imagine Wonder World Cave filled with water like this cave," said Mike. "But what I imagined doesn't come close to what I'm seeing in this video."

"Look," said Hannah. "The passageway is getting narrower." The camera showed an opening that looked quite small. The diver approached the opening.

Sarah gasped. "He's not going to try to go through it, is he? Oh, no! He'll never get through that narrow tunnel."

The four held their breaths as the diver started through the opening. The two tanks on his back were scraping the top of the tunnel.

"Oh, my gosh!" said Mike. "He can't get through. I think he's stuck. I never thought of myself as truly claustrophobic, but I'm changing my mind. No way could I do what he's doing."

They watched in fascination as the diver finally wriggled his way through the opening.

"Whew," said Mike. "Glad that's over. Of course, now he has to come through again on his way back."

"Look," said Luis. "He's pointing the camera all around the cave. That cave looks big."

"Yeah," said Mike. "It's a big room with a ceiling about twelve feet high."

The film ended and Mike began to rewind it. "We've collected some good material for our science report. Don't you guys agree that we can begin to pull our report together now?"

"As far as I am concerned, we can begin the report," said Hannah. "Sarah, have you gotten all the pictures developed?"

"Yes, but I am not the world's best photographer. Some of them are blurry and some didn't have enough light. I do have some really pretty ones of the well itself, though. And a couple of great ones of you guys in the well."

"We forgot about pictures of Wonder Cave," said Luis.

"I bought some postcards in the gift shop," said Hannah. "They show some of the rooms and one is a picture of the different kinds of rock."

"That reminds me," said Mike. "I bought some samples of the rock types."

"If we make a display of the pictures, postcards, and rocks and put it with the written report and our map of Jacob's Well, we should have a really good report worked up," said Luis. "Mike, are you working on the written part?"

"Yeah, but there are a lot of loose ends yet. Don't forget that you guys each have a section of the report to write up."

"I have been thinking about our report," Sarah said, "and I have an idea for part of our presentation if you guys want to do it. We could make a midden."

"Make a what?" asked Luis, a quizzical look on his face.

"A midden. It's where archaeologists find a lot of the artifacts. Really it's just an ancient trash pile," Sarah explained. "We could make a Tonkawa midden. We would let several students have a *dig* right there in class."

"That's a great idea, Sarah," said Hannah. "We could use a shallow plastic tub filled with sand. I think we have the right sized tub in our garage. But what could we bury in it?"

"Well, let's all think about that," answered Sarah. "To start with, a piece of charcoal could show they had fire and cooked their food. A piece of broken pottery would be good."

Hannah spoke up. "Mike, you love barbecued ribs. Save a couple of those rib bones to go in the midden. We'll probably think of other things before we actually make the midden."

"We need an arrowhead," said Luis. "Why don't we borrow the one we found at Jacob's Well?"

"We can't do that," said Sarah. "We promised David we would leave any artifacts right where we found them. That's why we were so careful about the arrowhead we found."

"We wouldn't be taking it to keep," said Mike. "We can put it right back after we give our report."

"Okay," said Sarah. "But I still think it's a bad idea."

"I don't like it either," said Hannah. "But a real arrowhead sure would be good to have in the midden."

"That's decided, then," said Mike. "We'll get the arrowhead just before we make the midden so it won't get lost."

"Don't forget, you guys," reminded Sarah, "we still have mysteries to solve. When I heard the guitar music that night, I really thought it was a ghost, but in the cold light of day, I knew better. Now I am ready to figure out where it came from."

Sarah was quiet for a minute. "Do you think somebody from school was trying to play a trick on us?"

"No way," answered Luis. "We didn't even know

we would be out there that night. How could any-body else know?"

"I have an idea," said Hannah. "The days are getting longer now. Maybe if we hang around the well in the late afternoons we might hear the music again. Mr. Bartle doesn't lock up until dark. We just might get lucky."

"Or unlucky, if we hear it and it's the ghost," joked Mike.

"It's worth a try," said Luis. "We can ride out after school every day. We could work some more on the path since we still haven't finished the part from the valley to the education center. Or we could do some of our homework if we need to."

"Let's ride out together every day and see what happens," said Sarah.

CHAPTER 22
Tracking the Music

"I figure we are about halfway from the valley to the education center," said Luis, adding another rock to the path. "You know," he added thoughtfully, "we have done a pretty good job for just the four of us. When we started this whole project, I was afraid we would never stick with it this long. But it really has been fun and we have had our own private swimming hole. You can't beat that."

"Mike," asked Hannah, "didn't David tell you that when the rocks are lined up on both sides of the path, other volunteers plan to line the path with cedar chips?"

"That's right," answered Mike. "We are invited to help with that part of the project, too."

"Well, why not," said Sarah. "I really want to be in on all these improvements as they take place. I understand the Preserve committee plans to make a nature walk out of this and teach groups about the plants and trees."

"I like that," said Hannah. "This will be a field trip for little school kids. Then when we go off to college, there will be some little squirts all trained to take our place."

"*Hmm*, Hannah. Sounds like you plan to be part of this place until you graduate," said Mike. "Good idea."

"Everybody, shhh!" cautioned Luis. "Listen."

"It's the music!" whispered Sarah. "And it's coming from that direction." She pointed to an area far from the creek. "Let's follow the sound. Come on!"

Following Sarah, they made their way through the thick underbrush. "This is tough going," she said softly, "but I think we are getting closer. Let's stop and listen a minute."

They paused and stood quietly. "It's still playing," whispered Hannah. "Let's keep going."

Branches from the stubby cedars scratched at their bare legs as they pushed on through the brush, still damp from a morning shower. It was hot, sweaty work, and progress was slow. "Stop a minute," said Luis. "I still hear the music and it sounds closer. But I thought I also heard thunder."

"That's all we need," grumbled Sarah. "Oh, no,"

she wailed. She stopped suddenly, almost causing a collision with Hannah, who was following close behind her.

"What?" asked Hannah, regaining her balance.

"The thunder," Sarah said, ominously. "That means rain, and rain means the ghost of Gray Wolf could come."

"Sarah, you don't really believe that stuff, do you?" asked Luis.

"Well, Mike and Sarah's Great Uncle Ezra said he and his friend saw the ghost and I don't think he would have lied. And those campers saw it, too. And they described it the same way Great Uncle Ezra did."

"Yeah, I guess they must have seen something," Luis agreed. "And it sure scared them."

Thunder rumbled in the distance. Even Mike was beginning to feel an uneasiness that made the hair on the back of his neck stand up. "We'd better hurry," he said to the others.

They continued through the brush, startling several deer into a run. "The music's closer," said Mike. "We're getting there. Wonder what we will find."

"From the sound of that thunder, we'll find us some rain pretty soon," said Hannah. "I don't like it."

"Look," said Sarah as the others caught up to

her. "Look there in that clearing. It's some kind of cabin. And that's where the music is coming from." They could hear the melody from a guitar quite clearly now.

"That's it!" exclaimed Luis excitedly. "I think I know who's playing the guitar. It's Wimberley Willie!"

"How can you be so sure that's who it is?" asked Hannah.

"Remember when we were eating ice cream at the deli and I told you there was something almost at the front of my mind, that it was like a question was answered, but I didn't know what the question was? Remember?"

"I remember that," said Mike. "I thought you were a little nuts."

"Well," continued Luis. "Now I know what was bothering me. Willie's music was familiar, the same music we heard in the woods that night."

"There goes our ghost," said Hannah.

"Yeah, thank goodness," Sarah said. "Come on, let's go talk to him."

They approached the small one-room building, but saw no one. The shabby house looked even smaller up close. Its rough unpainted boards and tumble-down appearance gave it a deserted look.

"Hello," called Mike.

The rough-hewn door of the shack opened slowly. Guitar in hand, a large man dressed in a torn T-shirt and jeans appeared at the door of the shack. His unkempt hair was long and stringy and matched his untrimmed beard. Meeting their gaze with steely gray eyes, he asked in a gravelly voice, "What do you kids want?"

"Uh, we don't mean to bother you," answered Mike, "but we have been working on the path back in the woods and we heard your guitar music and we . . . we thought we'd come investigate."

Wimberley Willie said nothing, continuing to stare at the four young people.

Luis spoke up. "We saw you in town not long ago. Is this where you live?"

"A man's got to live somewhere," was the gruff answer.

"We like your music," spoke Sarah, timidly. "Would you play some more for us?" she asked.

"Well, I don't know why not, little lady," he answered in a more friendly tone. "I guess I could do that. Just sit on them rocks over there and we'll have us a little music get-together right here and now."

And with that, Willie began to play, fingers flying, music filling the air. Hannah couldn't sit still. With her foot tapping in time to the music, she soon was clapping her hands, caught up in the rhythm and beat of the music.

Luis, Mike, and Sarah joined in. A smile crossed Willie's face as he watched them.

He finished the song. "Well, now, this is right nice. I don't get much company way out here in the woods. So ya'll are welcome anytime. But now, it feels like we're about to have a big rain storm so I think you better get back to wherever you came from." With that, he turned, walked back through the door of the shack, and shut the door.

"Well, what do you know!" exclaimed Luis, turning around to start back toward the creek. "We just met Wimberley Willie."

"Or whoever he really is," said Sarah. "We didn't even find out his real name."

"He invited us to come back so maybe we can visit him some more and learn more about him," said Mike.

The four began to make their way through the brush. The sky had darkened, and a few raindrops filtered through the leaves. The woods that usually seemed so welcoming and friendly now seemed menacing and threatening. Low branches of trees seemed to clutch at them as the wind grew stronger and moved the small trees back and forth.

"What's that?" cried Sarah, hearing a loud snap, then a crash. "It's somebody in the woods."

"No, Sarah, it's just a dead limb that broke off and fell," said Luis.

"Well, at least it's not foggy and that's what Gray Wolf likes. He only comes in fog," Sarah said aloud to reassure herself.

The raindrops had turned into a light mist. The four friends were nearing the cliff overlooking the well.

"Thank goodness," said Hannah as they came to the cliff top. Suddenly, the four of them stopped as one, not believing the sight that met them. A low fog hung over the creek and well. Misty tentacles rose from the scene below. A wavering shape rose from the rock where Gray Wolf's ghost had stood.

Sarah stifled a scream. "It's the ghost!" she said in a voice filled with terror. "It's the ghost!"

"No, Sarah, it's not a ghost. It's only fog," said Mike, unconvincingly.

"Let's go back," urged Hannah. "Gray Wolf's rock is right at the bottom of the cliff steps. We have to walk right over it."

"We'll have to walk right through his ghost," wailed Sarah. "I can't do that!"

"Now, everybody," said Luis, "calm down. First,

look down there at the rock. Do you actually see a ghost? Is an American Indian standing on the rock? Is anybody standing down there waving for us to come close?"

"Well, no," answered Sarah meekly.

"All right, then," said Luis. "What we have here is fog, just plain old fog. That often happens over bodies of water in weather like this, right, Mike?"

"Right," said Mike.

"Right, Hannah?" asked Luis.

"Right," said Hannah. "Come on, Sarah, let's go first. Follow me down the cliff steps, but be careful. They may be slippery."

Hannah and Sarah led the way down the wet steps toward Gray Wolf's rock at the bottom. The fog was heavier at the bottom of the cliff and Hannah could easily believe the ghost was waiting there for them, beckoning for them to come closer.

Gulping back her fear, she took Sarah's hand and together they stepped through the fog. "Keep your eyes down so you won't step into the well," she told Sarah as they crossed the haunted rock.

Moments later they were on the banks of the creek, the boys close behind them.

"We made it!" said Sarah, with relief.

"And no ghost—well, no ghost today, anyway," said Luis.

In a few minutes they were riding down the misty road and on their way home.

CHAPTER 23
The Warning

Several days later, the four were once again out at Jacob's Well. They were still marking the path with rocks, a job which was now nearing completion. "Let's quit for a while and go see if Willie is home," suggested Hannah.

"Good idea," said Luis. Soon they were approaching Willie's shack.

"Hey, it's us," called Mike. "Are you home?"

The door to the shack opened and Willie came out. "Well, hello there, young folks. Come for another visit, eh? Have a seat."

The kids sat down on the large rocks near the shack. "Uh, sir," began Mike, "we've been wondering what your name is. The folks in town call you Wimberley Willie. Is your name really Willie?"

"Sort of," answered Willie. "My name is William. When I was a boy I was called Bill by most folks.

Some called me Will and some called me Willie, so I guess that's where the Wimberley Willie comes from. Willie's fine with me, so that's what you can call me. Say, you kids find any arrowheads out here?" Willie asked.

"We sure did," answered Sarah, "but we know we are supposed to leave them where we find them." She didn't want Willie to know they were even thinking about taking the arrowhead to class.

"Right thing to do, leaving them where they are," said Willie, tugging on his beard. "Lots of people take whatever artifacts they find. They don't seem to know they are taking a piece of history away from where it belongs."

"Do you kids know what kind of American Indians once lived out here in these parts?" Willie asked.

Mike answered, "I was told that they were the Tonkawa tribe, but we don't know anything about the Tonkawas except that they were a friendly tribe."

"That's right," said Willie. "At least they were friendly with lots of the neighboring tribes. They did steal horses sometimes from the white men settling in these parts and that caused a lot of bad feeling.

"The Tonkawas used to be a big tribe," continued Willie. "They were spread out all around these parts. Then the Comanches moved in and squeezed the Tonkawa tribe into a smaller area."

"Did the Tonkawas live in teepees?" asked Sarah.

"Yep," answered Willie, "in teepees, huts, and wickiups."

"Wickiups?" asked Hannah. "What is a wickiup?"

"It's kinda hard to describe," Willie said. "They took branches that would bend easily and wove them into a sort of dome shape. Then they covered the dome with skins and leafy branches. Made a pretty good house.

"Here's something else interesting about the Tonkawas," added Willie. "They used dogs to transport their belongings. They would strap buffalo and deer hides to the dogs when they went to trade the hides to the white settlers."

"What did the Tonkawas eat?" asked Sarah.

"Well, they always tried to live near streams so they could catch fish. Back then there were big crawfish in the creeks, too, and those made good eating. And there were freshwater clams and mussels."

"What about animals?" asked Luis. "Did they eat meat?"

"They sure did," answered Willie. "And there was plenty of it back then—buffalo, deer, rabbits, squirrels, turtles. Sometimes they even ate rats and skunks. And rattlesnake."

"Ugh," said Sarah. "I don't think I could ever get hungry enough to eat a rat or a skunk."

"Or rattlesnake meat, either," said Hannah.

"I ate some rattlesnake meat when I lived in Mexico," said Luis. "It was pretty good, actually. It tasted a lot like chicken."

"Willie," asked Mike, "have you ever heard anything about the ghost of Gray Wolf?"

"Oh, sure," said Willie, "but I've never seen him. Always kind of hoped I would."

"If there really is a ghost, why do you think he hangs around at the well?" asked Luis.

"I've thought about that a lot. There's no way to know, of course, but I think he's kind of guarding the place."

Willie continued. "This whole place was so fresh and clean and undisturbed when the Tonkawas came. Now people take the arrowheads or whatever they find. Sometimes they even leave trash behind when they picnic. They let chemicals wash into the creek. I think old Gray Wolf just wants them to take care of the place."

"Why would he beckon for people to come closer?" asked Sarah.

"Ah, now, I've thought about that a lot, too," Willie replied. "I believe old Gray Wolf's got a secret to share with us," Willie said mysteriously.

"A secret?" asked Hannah.

"Yep," said Willie. "Maybe some day we'll know what the secret is."

Then Willie asked abruptly, "You know what the word Tonkawa means?"

Before anyone could answer, Willie said, "Some say it means they all stay together. Others say it means the people of the wolf."

Willie continued. "The Tonkawas believed their first ancestor was a wolf. Not a real wolf, but a mythical one. So they would never kill a wolf. Wolves and coyotes both were believed by the Tonkawas to be sacred."

Luis's eyes grew big. "Maybe that was a wolf we heard in the woods." With a twinkle, he added, "Or maybe it was the ghost of a Tonkawa imitating a wolf."

"You saying you heard some kind of animal noise in the woods?" Willie asked.

"Yes," said Hannah, "but when we heard the sounds of a mountain lion on the Internet, we decided that's what it was. Have you ever heard of any mountain lions around here?"

"Seen 'em," Willie replied. "Seen 'em not too

long ago—a mother mountain lion with her two cubs. Pretty sight."

"That's another mystery solved then," said Mike. "That really was a mountain lion we heard."

"Why do you live out here in the woods by yourself?" asked Luis.

"That's a long story, boy," answered Willie. "It's one I'd rather not tell right now." A look of sadness came into his eyes and he sat in deep thought for a few minutes.

He looked at the four of them, his face stern. "You kids been swimming in the well, right?"

"Yes, we have," answered Sarah.

"Don't!" Willie answered with a sudden fierceness. "I'm telling you, don't do it! There's danger there!" He rose, went into the shack, and slammed the door.

"Strange man," commented Mike as they left the clearing.

"He is sort of weird," agreed Hannah. "But I like him. And he sure knows a lot of interesting things."

CHAPTER 24
Danger in the Well

On a hot Saturday afternoon, Hannah suggested they ride out to the well and pick up the arrowhead.

"Good idea," said Mike. "Then we can go swimming in the well."

In spite of Willie's strange warning, the friends continued to swim in the well. After they had tramped through the woods to pick up the arrowhead, which Mike had put in his pocket, they were ready to cool off in the well.

"Where are you going?" Mike asked as Luis went into the thicket where they had hidden their bikes.

"Gotta get something," answered Luis. He soon returned with swim fins and a face mask. "I am going to try to go deeper."

"Luis, I wish you wouldn't do that," warned Mike. "It really bothers me."

"Yeah, Luis," said Sarah. "Remember Willie's warning. He said the well is dangerous."

"Oh, he's just weird," said Luis, pulling on his bright blue swim fins. Somewhere deep inside himself, Luis knew his friends were right. He had no business taking any kind of chance in the well. But every time he swam in its cold clear waters, he felt a stronger compulsion to explore more of it. It was as though the well had cast a spell over him.

Luis started to put on his face mask. Sarah grabbed his arm. "Luis," she begged, "please, please don't dive down there. So many people have died in this well. Please don't go deep. Something terrible will happen. I just know it will."

Luis turned his face to Sarah, but his eyes had a strange, glazed, faraway look. Sarah knew he had not really heard her plea.

"Mike, do something. Stop him!" Sarah was shouting now, but Luis slowly turned back toward the well, an eerie smile on his face, his ears deaf to her begging.

Mike reached for Luis's arm, but before he could touch it, Luis pulled away from Sarah's grasp and propelled himself down into the opening of the well.

Mike, Sarah, and Hannah watched helplessly as

the blue fins waving in the clear water went deeper and deeper.

Luis swam straight down. *This time I am going to the bottom. I can do it. I can do anything,* he thought elatedly. A feeling of power swept over him and he felt that a watery ally was pulling him down, down. It was so easy!

I'm so near the bottom, Luis decided. *I'll pick up a rock from the floor of the well and take it back up. I'll show them. I can do anything!* Luis was convinced nothing could happen to him in the depths of the well. He was safe, wrapped in the icy arms of some invisible, embracing, watery creature.

He reached for a stone on the bottom of the pit.

No, no, go back. Go back, said a small voice from somewhere in his mind. *Go back now.*

Suddenly, Luis felt as though he had been awakened from a dream. He turned quickly to head for the surface. He could see the light of the opening above him, so far away. Too far away. He experienced a fear so strong that he had never felt anything like it; he could not have imagined anything like it. Horror and panic overwhelmed him. His lungs ached. He was suffocating. He would drown.

On the surface at the rim of the well, Sarah was screaming. "Luis, Luis! Oh, God, please, Luis, come up."

"Help! Somebody, please help us," shouted Hannah.

"I'll go for help," said Mike.

The well in front of them suddenly erupted in a geyser of icy water.

"It's Willie," shouted Hannah. "He's dived into the well. He must have heard us."

Down below, Luis, nearing unconsciousness, felt the vibration of a splash. Strong hands quickly grabbed him and shot him to the surface.

Only moments later, Luis was stretched out on the warm ground, taking deep breaths and glorying in the sight of tree tops and blue sky and sunshine.

"Good gosh, Luis," said Hannah. "You just about scared us to death. If it hadn't been for Willie..." She began to cry. "We were so scared."

Luis reached a hand out to Willie. "Willie, I don't know what to say. You saved my life. Thank you."

"It's okay, kid," said Willie, grasping Luis's hand briefly. "Gotta go," and he climbed the cliff and disappeared into the woods.

— CHAPTER 25 —
The Midden

Hannah, Mike, Sarah, and Luis were gathered around the kitchen table.

"Let's see," said Hannah. "We've got the plastic tub all ready. I wish it were something more rustic. A plastic tub sure wouldn't be found in a Tonkawa midden. Oh, well, I guess it'll have to do."

"Here's the sand," said Luis. "I got it from a builder friend of my parents. I hope it will be enough."

"Oh, it'll be fine," said Sarah. "I just wish we had more artifacts. Let's see, we've got the ribs, a clam shell, a piece of charcoal, a wishbone from a turkey, some nuts in their shells, a piece of broken pottery, and of course, the arrowhead. It would be nice if we could put in some fish bones, but they would break too easily."

Only the arrowhead was left to put in the midden. They all looked at the arrowhead. "Are you thinking the same thing I am?" asked Mike. "That maybe what happened at the well with Luis was because we had just taken the arrowhead?"

"Yeah," said Hannah. "That's exactly what I was thinking, so I say that as soon as we finish giving our report, we put that arrowhead back where it belongs."

"Can't be soon enough for me," said Luis. "I, for one, don't need any more scary things like what happened to me in the well."

The next day the four ate lunch together in the school cafeteria. Science class was right after lunch, so they left the cafeteria early to prepare their presentation in the science classroom. Mike arranged the rocks, pictures, and other items on a table at the front of the room. The girls began putting together the midden.

"Let's put the arrowhead on the very bottom, since that's our only real artifact," suggested Sarah. "That way, maybe they will find it last and add a little drama to that part of our presentation."

"Good idea," agreed Hannah. They placed the arrowhead in a corner of the tub, then poured sand over it. Next came the ribs covered by more sand. The other items were layered with sand, and the midden was ready for the presentation.

"Well, I guess we're ready," said Mike. "We'll each read our part of the report. Then we can show them the pictures and rocks and the map we made."

"And last, we do the activity with the midden," said Sarah. "Let's choose volunteers to come up and dig out an item. Then they can tell us what that item tells them about how the Tonkawas lived."

Just about that time, the first students—followed by Mrs. Jameson, their teacher—entered the classroom.

When everyone was seated and quiet, Mrs. Jameson said, "Class, one of our research groups has prepared a presentation for you, so I am going to ask Mike to begin and tell us a little about their project."

Mike stepped forward and explained the object of their study. "We have each prepared a part of the presentation, so I will read my report first. My part is about the cave at San Marcos."

Mike shared with the class the information they had found about Wonder Cave and told them a little about their adventure in the dark.

Luis then gave his report about Jacob's Well and had the class listening intently as he told them about the dangers of the well and about his own near-tragedy at the bottom of the well.

Hannah was next and shared with the class information about how to prevent pollution of Jacob's Well and Cypress Creek and how to care for the area around the well.

"I hope you will all go out to the well the next time they have the Jacob's Well Festival," said Hannah. "You can see for yourself what we have done and what a beautiful place it is and why we must work hard to preserve it."

Sarah stood up next and read her report about the Tonkawa tribe. She also told them about the ghost, knowing she would have no trouble keeping their attention with the story of Gray Wolf.

Then she walked over to the plastic tub. "You may know," she said, "what a midden is, but for those of you who might not know, I will explain it." She gave her explanation of a real midden, then pointed to the plastic tub. "This will be our midden."

Sarah then asked two students to come forward. She said to them, "We thought a couple of you might enjoy being archaeologists for a few minutes. With a little imagination, this is a Tonkawa midden. We invite you to go on an archeological dig in our midden.

"When you find an artifact, please explain to us what you think that artifact tells you about the Tonkawa tribe."

The first student dug around in the sand and

pulled out the wishbone. "Well," the student said, looking at the wishbone in her hand, "this is a pretty big wishbone, so I think it must have come from a turkey. I believe turkey was one of the foods the Tonkawas ate."

The class applauded. One by one, the items were pulled from the sand until at last, nothing more could be found. The student who had been digging started to his seat.

"Wait," called Sarah, "there is one more item. It is the most important one of all. Dig again."

Once more the student dug around in the tub. He found nothing.

Sarah paled. "But there is an arrowhead in there. We put it over in this corner." She stuck her hand in the tub and dug into every corner and all over the bottom, sifting sand through her fingers." There was nothing but sand. Sarah returned to her seat looking crushed.

Mrs. Jameson thanked them. "That was an excellent and unique presentation. We have learned a lot and appreciate all the trouble you have gone to in sharing your knowledge with us all."

As soon as class was over, Sarah, Hannah, Mike, and Luis clustered together in the hall.

"You helped me do the midden, Hannah, and

you saw exactly where I placed the arrowhead. The midden was never out of our sight. Where could the arrowhead have gone?"

"Somebody who was digging in the midden must have pocketed it," said Luis.

"No, I am positive that didn't happen," said Sarah. "I watched every movement they made and saw every object that was pulled from that tub. I was so anxious that the arrowhead be the last thing pulled up that I didn't take my eyes off that tub. I saw every last grain of sand that even moved."

Hannah said, "I am trying hard to think of some logical explanation, but I am lost this time. It's just too weird."

"I knew all along Gray Wolf wouldn't want us to take that arrowhead. Now I've gone and lost it." Sarah was almost in tears.

"Don't worry, Sarah," said Luis. "The arrowhead will turn up." But he didn't believe a word of what he was saying. He kept thinking about old Gray Wolf and his ghost guarding Jacob's Well to keep people from doing things like stealing artifacts.

CHAPTER 26
Willie Revealed

A week later, the four friends sat at a table in the shade of a huge oak tree growing beside the pizza restaurant. Luis opened a pizza box. "Help yourselves," he told Hannah, Mike, and Sarah. "I bought two large ones so we have plenty of pizza."

They all took pieces and began to enjoy the hot, cheesy taste of the pizza.

"Feels good to have our report done and turned in, doesn't it?" asked Mike. "Pizza is a good way to celebrate."

"Yes," agreed Hannah. "And I think we did a good job."

"Except for the disappearing arrowhead," said Sarah. "I still feel guilty about it. It sure is a mystery."

"Say, I almost forgot," added Mike. "I wanted to tell you what I found out about Willie. Do you know

Mr. Avery, the old guy who has the woodworking shop at the end of the square downtown?"

"You mean that old man who always wears a leather vest?" asked Hannah. "The one we see sometimes at the deli?"

"Yeah, that's the one," her brother answered. "I was in the deli the other day and started talking to him. I figured he'd probably been around Wimberley longer than anybody else, so I asked him about Wimberley Willie.

"Mr. Avery says that years and years ago, Willie was just a normal kind of guy. His hobby was diving. But he had a bad diving experience."

Mike drank some of his root beer, then continued. "Willie and his buddy were doing a dive in Jacob's Well and Willie's buddy went down to the third cave, really deep. Something happened down there with his air tank and nobody else could get deep enough to find him.

"Willie kept going out to the well, diving to hunt for his friend's body. Of course, he took other people with him to help, but Willie felt that somehow it was his fault. He believed that he should be the one to find his friend and bring his body to the surface. Willie finally found his friend." Mike became very quiet.

"Are you telling us that the picture you showed

us was Willie's friend?" asked Luis. "And the other person in the picture was Willie?"

"I'm afraid so. Mr. Avery said after that happened, Willie just kind of went weird, quit his job, and moved out to that shack. Willie told people back then that he had to stay near the well. Nobody understood why and nobody understands why today. But that's why Willie lives out there all by himself."

"And that's why he warned us about swimming in the well. We should have listened to him," said Sarah.

"Yeah," said Luis. "And after what happened to me in Jacob's Well, I'm beginning to understand why that place is not a public park, open for everybody. I know people sneak in to swim sometimes, but if they had been through what I did, they'd go find a public pool somewhere! It's not worth risking your life."

Luis chewed thoughtfully on a bite of pizza. "There is something so strange about that well. You must think I'm crazy, but it was like somebody had hypnotized me or cast a magic spell on me."

"We believe you, Luis," said Sarah. "I only wish we had done more to stop you from trying to dive so deep."

"I'm just grateful it's all over and I'm alive and well. And ready, by the way, to go back out to the well," said Luis.

"No way any of us will go back into that well anytime soon. Forget that," said Mike forcefully.

"No, I didn't mean go into the well again. I want to go back out there and see if we can figure out the mystery of the message on the stone," Luis said.

"What's the point?" asked Hannah. "We tried everything and had to give up. I don't mind going out to finish our work on the path, but it's a waste of time to fool with that stone anymore."

"I agree," said Mike. "Let's forget the stone. But let's do plan to keep working on the path. We need to get it finished."

—— CHAPTER 27 ——
Unraveling the Mystery

After several more visits to Jacob's Well, the four partners had almost finished the path. Neat rows of rocks lined both sides. When the chipped cedar was laid down, it would be an attractive and inviting path through the woods.

Sarah lugged yet another large stone to the line of rocks marching alongside the path. "Whew," she said as she dropped the stone in line with the others. "I feel really good about what we have done. This has been a much bigger project than I thought it would be. But it is worth it."

"Yes," agreed Hannah. "We have done a lot more than just pick up trash. We have really contributed something good to our community."

"Yeah, that's for sure," said Luis. "But that mystery stone bugs the heck out of me. I wish we could figure out the message."

"But we all agreed to forget about that stone," Mike reminded him.

"Let's go one more time and just look at the stone," begged Luis. "I really want to see it one more time."

"Okay. One more time," said Mike.

They all followed Luis off the path to the site of the stone. On top of the leaf-covered mystery stone lay the triangular piece of rock they had left to mark the spot.

Luis removed the triangular rock and brushed the leaves away from the carved flat stone beneath it.

"Herein lies the secret 50N 20E 14S," Sarah read the stone aloud. "It's as big a puzzle as ever," she sighed.

Silently they stood looking at the stone when Hannah, breaking the silence, cried out, "I've got it. I think I have figured it out. Do you guys have the compass and tape measure with you?"

"Sure," answered Mike, pointing to a spot across the path, "right over there in my backpack. But tell us. What do you mean you have figured it out?"

"Okay, it's like this," Hannah answered excitedly. "Do you remember our punctuation lesson last week in English class? The one on commas?"

Luis looked at the others and grimaced. "She's

lost it now for sure," he said to Sarah and Mike. To Hannah he said, "I sure don't see what commas have to do with the stone."

"Here's how I see it," explained Hannah. "Remember the sentences Mrs. Langston gave us to show how commas can change the meaning of a sentence? They were something like this: When her mother called (comma) Mary Ann answered. When her mother called Mary (comma) Ann answered."

Hannah's friends stared at her blankly.

Hannah said impatiently. "See how it changes the meaning? Now look at the words on the stone. Suppose we put a comma after *Here* then another one after *lies*. Then the sentence reads, 'Here, in lies, the secret.'" Hannah expectantly watched her friends' faces, but they all looked baffled.

"You see," she explained further, "if the directions are lies, then maybe they are all the opposite of what it says. 50 north would really be 50 south, 20 east would be 20 west and 14 south would be 14 north."

"Hannah, you may have something there," said Luis. "It's wacky, but then this whole business of the stone is wacky. I say let's try it."

Mike walked over to his backpack that lay beside the path. He removed the measuring tape and compass and walked back to the stone. Just as he had done before, Mike held the compass, but this time held out his hand pointing to the south. Luis walked toward the south, while Hannah held the tape and Sarah stretched it toward Luis.

"This is fifty feet," Sarah called out. "I'm marking it."

The tape had taken them just past the east end of the valley. "Now to measure the twenty feet west," said Mike. They repeated the steps as before, but this time heading west.

"It's going to take us exactly parallel to the valley on the other side," shouted Luis.

Mike hurried to the spot at the end of the twenty feet. "Okay, this time we move fourteen feet north."

"Oops," said Sarah. "That takes us right down this steep hill toward the bottom of the valley. It's rocky and rough, but let's do it."

Once more Mike held the tape, Luis clambered down the hillside in a northerly direction, and Hannah and Sarah followed him, pulling the tape measure out to mark the last fourteen feet.

"Well, I'm here, at last," shouted Sarah. "But there is nothing here but a pile of rocks."

The others joined her at what appeared to be just

that—a pile of rocks on the steep side of the small valley. The rocks were partially covered with a vine.

"I'm so disappointed," said Hannah. "I was positive this was the answer."

CHAPTER 28
The Treasure

Sarah started back up the hill, stepping on the rocks in the pile. As she did, one of the rocks rolled downward, and Sarah slipped and fell on the rocky slope.

"Ouch," she cried. "I've skinned my knee and cut my hand. But I guess I'll live."

"Wait a minute," said Mike. "Look at this. There seems to be a hollow place behind that rock. Let's move some more rocks."

With new energy, they attacked the pile of rocks. "Look," shouted Luis, excitement in his voice. "It's a cave."

"Wow," said Sarah, "it sure is. Is it big enough for us to get in there?"

"Yeah," said Luis, "if we crawl in. Mike, let me use your flashlight."

"Okay," replied Mike, "but the battery is getting weak." Mike handed Luis the flashlight.

Luis crawled through the small opening. "Hey," he called back, "it's bigger once you get through the opening. I can even stand up. It's awesome. Hurry. Come on inside."

Quickly, the others followed Luis into the cave.

"Oh, this is really something," said Hannah, looking around. She brushed a spider web from her face. "It's spooky in here, like something from an old horror movie. But this must be where the treasure is."

"Luis, shine the light over here, quickly," Mike cried out.

Luis swung the beam of light to the wall near Mike. In the weakening beam of the flashlight were the outlines of an animal. "I think we have found our treasure," said Mike, a note of wonder in his voice. "Look at this."

Luis moved the spot of light closer to the place that Mike indicated on the wall. The others followed the beam of the flashlight.

Hannah gasped at what she saw. "It's a real cave drawing," she said softly, her voice filled with awe.

The flashlight dimmed and flickered, making the animal on the cave wall seem to move and come alive, its cold eyes staring at them across the years.

Sarah broke the silence. "What kind of animal is it?" she whispered.

"It looks like a wolf," said Luis. "The Tonkawas must have done it. It's probably thousands of years old."

"But if the Tonkawas did it," asked Sarah, "then why did somebody bury that stone with its mysterious message?"

"We can only guess at that," said Mike. "But I have an idea. Obviously there are no Tonkawas here today and there haven't been any here for maybe a couple of hundred years. I figure somebody who knew the last of the Tonkawas considered this painting a treasure and didn't want it trashed. At the same time, he wanted the painting to be found someday, maybe so it could be appreciated."

"I like that theory, Mike," said Luis.

"Let's go find Willie and then David and let them know about the treasure," suggested Hannah. "They'll find a way to share it with others and keep it protected, too."

The four friends left the cave and headed excitedly to Willie's shack to share the news.

"Willie, Willie," they all yelled at once as they neared the cabin. "We've got great news!"

The door of Willie's house creaked open and he stood at the door, his big body nearly filling the space in the doorway. A grin split his bearded face as he welcomed the four friends. "Well, you four must have discovered gold from the looks on your faces."

"It's better than gold," Mike said. "It's the best treasure you can imagine."

"Yes," echoed Sarah, clapping her hands excitedly. "You're not going to believe what a treasure we have found!"

Breathlessly taking turns, Mike, Hannah, Sarah, and Luis described what they had found in the cave.

"Sounds like you have found the real thing," agreed Willie. "The whole community is going to be excited about this. You young folks have done a real service for this area. David is probably at the education center now. I know you want him to see what you have found. Go get him, and I will meet you at the top of the valley. Hurry now."

David excitedly returned with them to the valley where Willie was waiting for them.

"I think the kids have really found something special," Willie said to David. "It was hard for me not to go ahead into the cave to see the drawing, but I thought you should see it first."

David had a big flashlight with him. He stooped to enter the cave and shone the light around until he saw the cave painting of the wolf. He gasped. "My gosh," they heard him say. "This is fantastic! And I am sure it's the real thing. Look, Willie," he said as Willie crowded into the cave with him.

"Wow," said Willie. "That's really something. It sure enough is a treasure."

They came back out into the sunlight. "We will get somebody from the university to authenticate this, but I am almost absolutely positive it's the real thing. This is an important archeological find and we have you kids to thank for it." David added, "I promise you right now, this cave will be protected and the cave painting will be preserved."

"We'd like that. We kind of feel like we owe it to the Tonkawa tribe and especially to Gray Wolf," said Mike.

"We'll be in touch with you," said David as he started back toward the education center with Willie, "and thanks again for everything you have done out here."

"Yeah," said Sarah softly to her friends, "like stealing the arrowhead. If you guys don't mind, I would like to stop on the way back to the creek and at least look at the spot where the arrowhead used to be."

"That will just make you feel worse, Sarah," said Hannah. "Why keep torturing yourself?"

"I know, it sounds dumb. But please, I just want to go move the rock and see the spot."

"Okay," said Mike. "It's on our way back, so it's no problem."

Soon they were near the place where Sarah had found the arrowhead. They left the path and walked to the large smooth stone which was still under the odd-shaped limb Hannah had placed over it. Hannah removed the limb and Sarah lifted the stone. She gasped. "Oh, no, I don't believe this. Look!"

Her three friends gathered around the place and looked down. "It can't be," said Hannah. "There's no way."

There, in the very same position they had first found it, lay the arrowhead.

"Sarah, had you told anybody about our finding the arrowhead here?"

"No, I never mentioned it to a soul. It was sort of fun to have a secret like that. And then later, I sure didn't want to tell anybody we stole it."

"Hannah, we didn't 'steal' it," said Mike. "We just borrowed it. But I never told anybody about it either. What about you, Luis?"

"Oh, no, not me," said Luis. "I was like Sarah. I thought it was just our secret."

"Then there's only one answer," said Sarah. "The ghost of Gray Wolf took it from the midden right there in the classroom and brought it back here."

The other three stood speechless.

"Can anybody think of a better explanation?" asked Sarah.

They shook their heads. "No, I guess not," said Mike.

"And you know what else?" said Sarah. "I'll bet the cave drawing was the ghost's secret. That's what he wanted to tell somebody, buy nobody was ever brave enough to get close to him."

"Sarah, I never thought I would say a thing like this about a ghost, but it makes sense to me," said Luis.

"Well, my friends," said Mike, as they made their way toward the education center. "It has been an eventful spring, wouldn't you say?"

Sarah, Luis, and Hannah nodded in agreement.

"Yes," repeated Mike, trudging through the now-familiar woods. "It's been quite a spring."

GLOSSARY

Algae: a simple form of plant life found in water

Apparition: a ghostly appearance

Apprehension: fear of future trouble

Aquifer: a body of porous rock which stores ground water

Archaeologist: one who studies the artifacts of ancient people to learn about their culture

Artifact: an object made by a human in ancient times

Blanco River: Texas river flowing from Blanco to San Marcos

Bobcat: an American wildcat

Boulders: large rounded or worn rocks

Calcite: calcium carbonate, a common mineral

Chert: a compact rock which is mostly quartz

Claustrophobic: fearful of enclosed or narrow places

Coliform: a bacteria which can cause serious illness

Comanche: an American Indian tribe that lived mostly in northern and western Texas

Compass: an instrument for determining directions

Compulsion: being strongly drawn to something against one's will

Conjure: bring to mind

Corpus Christi: large city on the Gulf Coast of Texas

Cotton Gin: machine to separate cotton fibers from cotton seeds

Coyote: a wolf-like animal

Crawfish: a small freshwater lobster

Crevice: a crack that forms an opening

Dig: an archeological site being excavated

Dolomite: a mineral, calcium magnesium carbonate or rock with this mineral in it

Ecology: study of the relationship between organisms and their environment

Eerie: weird

Elongated: lengthened

Emphatically: forcefully in speech

Endangered Species: animals or plants in danger of disappearing forever

Fault Line: dislocation along the fracture in a rock

Ferocious: savagely fierce

Focal Point: main point of interest

Foreboding: an inner certainty of a future misfortune

Geology: science dealing with the earth

Geyser: fountainlike jet of water shooting up into the air

Gnawing: continuing, persistent

Gristmill: a mill for grinding grain

Hazards: dangers or risks

Hypnotic: makes one feel sleepy or hypnotized

Illuminated: lighted

Iron Pyrite: a mineral which looks like gold ore

Irrational: without good reason

Jerusalem: the capital city of Israel

Limestone: a stone made of calcium carbonate

Loathsome: revolting, disgusting

Manuscripts: a document written by hand

Marine fossil: rock-like remains of sea creatures

Marooned: left in a deserted place without any resources

Menacing: threatening to cause evil

Midden: ancient trash heap

Mussel: a freshwater clam

Nocturnal: coming out or active at night

Ominous: threatening evil or harm

Orienteering: skill of finding one's way using a map and a compass

Parallel: lines going side-by-side in the same direction

Peril: exposure to danger

Rabbi: spiritual leader of a Jewish congregation

Reef: a ridge of rocks or sand, often made of coral

Rhythmic: with regular pulses or beats

Rimrocks: rock forming the boundary of a rise in the land

San Marcos: a small city in Central Texas

Sawmill: a place in which timber is sawed into planks and boards

Sentinel: a person who stands guard

Sinister: threatening evil

Sorghum Mill: a mill that crushes sorghum grain to make syrup

Stalactite: an icicle-like deposit hanging from the roof of a cave

Stalagmite: like a stalactite, but formed on the floor of a cave

Submerge: to sink or plunge under water

Talc: a soft mineral

Tectonic Plates: forces in the earth that cause movement of its crust

Teepee: a cone-shaped tent of the American Indians, covered in animal skins

Tentacles: feelers of an animal that serve as organs of touch

Tonkawa: an American Indian tribe which lived in the area of Austin and at Jacob's Well

Undulate: to move with a wavelike motion

Wickiup: a dome-shaped American Indian home made of branches and covered with skins

Wimberley: a small village on the Blanco River in Central Texas

Wonder World Park: an amusement and animal park featuring Wonder Cave and located in San Marcos, Texas

Yucatan: a peninsula in southeast Mexico and north Central America

BIBLIOGRAPHY

Burnett, Carolyn Mitchell. *The First Texans*. Austin, TX: Eakin Press, 1995.

Day, Joe. "Up the Creek Without a Well." Wimberley, TX: *Hometown News and Views*, Vol. 3, Issue 2, September 2000.

Madden, Janice, Martha Knies, Charlene Polansky. *Welcome to Wimberley, Now What Do I Do?* Wimberley, TX: The Cottage Press, 1993.

Schawe, Williedell (Editor). *Wimberley's Legacy*. Austin, TX: Eakin Press, 2000.

Thoene, Bodie & Brock. *Jerusalem Vigil*. New York, NY: Viking Press, 2000.

Wall, Bert M. *The Devil's Backbone*. Austin, TX: Eakin Press, 1999.

WEB SITES

The Tonkawa Indians. http://www.TexasIndians.com

Hill Country Critters. http://www.visitwimberley.com

Mammals of Texas—Online Edition. Texas Parks and Wildlife. http://www.tpwd.state.tx.us

Jacob's Well. Handbook of Texas Online. http://www.tsha.utexas.edu.handbook/online

San Marcos Area Recovery Team. http://www.corridor.net/smartdivers

Wonder World Park. http://www.wonderworldpark.com

After raising four children, **Marcia Allen Bennett** began a teaching career in Corpus Christi, Texas, where for fifteen years she worked closely with students in grades one through twelve as a teacher/librarian.

In addition to holding a bachelor of science degree from Corpus Christi State University and being certified as a teacher, she has fifteen hours toward a master's degree in Library Science from Sam Houston State University in Huntsville, Texas.

Six and a half years ago, Marcia and her attorney husband, Bill Bennett, moved to Wimberley in the Texas Hill Country, where they have enjoyed exploring the surrounding area and learning about its rich and colorful history.

Marcia's interests include woodcarving, building and playing folk instruments (hammered dulcimer, mountain dulcimer, Irish harp), building miniature furniture (selected as Artisan in International Guild of Miniature Artisans), reading, and quilting.

www.marciabennett.com